BACKSTORIES

ORDER OF THADDEUS • SHORT STORY COLLECTION 1

J. A. BOUMA

For my readers

INTRODUCTION

THE BACKSTORIES OF THEIR (AND OUR)
LIVES…

In December 2015 and into the early part of 2016, I began dreaming about writing an action-adventure religious thriller series that would take the best elements of some of my favorites in the genre.

I had been reading James Rollins and Steve Berry for years, loving their SIGMA and Magellan Billet fictional organizations that saved the world from no uncertain doom while plumbing the depths of questions dealing with science and history, with a touch of the philosophical and religious on the side. I also enjoyed the kinds of religious conspiracy yarns written by Dan Brown that explored deeper questions, while turning an irritated eye toward the more fantastical Christian claims.

So I started to dream. Dreaming about a religious order that would preserve the memory of the vintage Christian faith. Dreaming about those who would seek to destroy that memory, the powerful forces that would stop at nothing to obliterate the tangible and intangible expressions of that faith. And also a way to entertain and thrill, while inspiring for the journey and offering a dose of insight into faith along the way.

I still have my Moleskine notebook journal with some early ideas sketched. Here is what I wrote:

What if the Church had launched a secret order dedicated to preserving, protecting, struggling for the once-for-all faith, in the vein of Jude 3?

What if a project was launched to preserve the memory of the faith through objects and relics?

What if a secret organization was dedicated to the destruction of the memory of the Christian faith and Church generally?

What if an ex-military professor was asked by the Vatican to join the project to preserve the relic memory of the vintage Christian faith?

Thus was born the Order of Thaddeus and Project SEPIO! As well as the heroes that were part of the Order and that project.

Can't remember entirely now how they came about, but early on I had the main protagonist name: Silas Grey. I think I liked what his last name symbolized: the space between black and white, faith and doubt, right and wrong, hope and despair. I knew he was ex-military, serving during the post-9/11 years after his dad was killed in the Pentagon during the attacks. He was a professor of religious studies and church history, a badass and troublemaker. And he was an expert on the Shroud of Turin, the first relic of the vintage Christian faith that drew him into the storyline of my first book in the series, *Holy Shroud*.

Celeste Bourne came next, her own last name sort of significant, a nod to the famous action hero. I wanted it to signal the strength and intrigue and power she had as a woman, whose background was with the British government's MI6 unit and who could hold her own against the most villainous of bad guys. Her storyline evolved as I continued writing the series, from her experiences with the occult to the death of her fiancé.

Same for Matt Gapinski and Naomi Torres and Rowen Radcliffe.

Every story needs the wise-old soul who comes alongside the crew with guidance and expertise, and maybe a little finger-wagging at times to get them to shape up. Sort of a trope of these kinds of books but also a valuable character, which Rowen Radcliffe fulfilled for a time. If you've been reading for a while, you know where his character goes, and the next chapter that change signaled.

You also need comic relief when the bullets are flying. Someone to offer a wisecrack or say the thing one normally only thinks of in their head when you need to breathe after a battle. That's Matt Gapinski, who was patterned a bit after James Rollins's character Joe Kowalski. (Sometimes we writers do that sort of thing!) I was asked once which of my characters I identify with most. Gapinski ranks up there, mostly because of his snark but also because he has endured his share of hardship and heartbreak.

Naomi Torres didn't come until the third book, and only then was meant as a one-off character for Hidden Covenant. But I loved how she and Gapinski interacted so much so that I carried her forward into every book to form my 4-person squad of faith-protectors! I also loved the backstory I discovered as I wrote her, and how her struggled at times to live her faith and understand it often reflect our own authentic struggles to do the same.

That's the thing with storytelling, or with the way I storytell at least: These characters come alive through the act itself. They are living, breathing people, friends really, who emerge from the page through the act of creation. Never really know what they're going to do or who they are until their stories unfold. And just like each of us, these characters, these friends, each have a backstory.

I've touched on these elements from their pasts in various

ways across the ten books (and counting!). But I thought it would be fun to explore these backstories more fully, telling the deeper background in short story form through their own first-person eyes.

So here you go: five stories from four characters that reveal their journeys through faith, life, and everything in-between—as much as they do about our own stories. Perhaps I will touch on other characters in other collections—like Sebastian Grey, Rowen Radcliffe, and the newest member Victor Zarruq—but this collection brings the spotlight on Silas, Celeste, Torres, and Gapinski.

The first short story is from Silas—naturally, my main hero. He and his best friend, Colton Green, find themselves on a return trip in Iraq to a village playing the part of community-relations manager for Uncle Sam—when something unexpected happens. I've recounted this story a few times in the series, so it made sense to unfold it in full here.

The second comes from Naomi Torres. It explores both a high and low point in her life, resulting in a family betrayal. Thankfully, that relational breech was mended during an important operation in one of my full-length novels, but here I explored what happened to lead to the split in the first place. It's a complicated story, one we all can relate to at some level when we ask ourselves why we do the things we do—especially the things that hurt others, and ourselves.

Story three comes from Silas's right-hand woman, Celeste Bourne. She tells the story from a part of her past she would rather have left undiscovered—but came to light in my seventh book, *Rite of Darkness*. This piece of her story was entirely unexpected when I wrote that book—yeah, those things happen! But it fit what unfolded in their lives, and I wanted to explore it more fully through her eyes.

The fourth story is told by Matt Gapinski's. Again, through his eyes, but different from the others: this time he is retelling a part of his past to a special someone in the future, and wondering how they will react. It's a mixture of heart-warm and gut-wrenching tragedy, given the part of his story he tells. Another one of those pieces I didn't see coming until he shared it with Silas in an adventure.

Finally, we return to Silas. It comes a few months after the first story, when he is grappling with the fallout from that fateful day. Along the way, he stumbles upon a religious service that draws him in. Can't help himself. And what happens next is wholly unexpected.

I published the first story in my series 36 months after I first started sketching those early details. Took me a bit to write book one, then some more time editing and polishing it for publication. I could never have imagined the reception the series has had over the past few years—consistently staying on the bestseller lists on Amazon for religious fiction and elsewhere, often launching as a number one new release, garnering mostly positive and enthusiastic reviews. The notes from readers thanking me for the books and letting me know how they've encouraged their own faith-journey on top of just plain entertaining them and offering an escape have made it more than worth it.

So thank you, dear reader, for my own author journey so far. This book is dedicated to you for making what I do possible. I hope these deeper dives into the lives of your favorite characters entertain and inspire for the journey. Perhaps more still: May you find glimpses of your own story in their backstories.

Grace and peace,

~J. A. Bouma (January 2021)

1. SILAS WEPT (SILAS GREY)

I t felt like it was going to be one of those days. The kind when the world spins one way and you go another. Like one of those playground carousels whirling and twirling —and you lose your grip and go tipping backward out of orbit, flying into the ground, dirt and wood chips getting stuffed up your nose and in your mouth, your taste buds getting a dose of what earthworms taste every day.

Last time I'd been thrown from life's carousel was when Dad died. Only then, the entire world spun out of orbit thanks to those damn Islamic whack jobs using their religion as justification to bring America to its knees. Those two planes slammed into the World Trade Center that fateful morning, and the world wasn't the same again. Then the one going down in that field in Pennsylvania thanks to a "Let's roll" rallying cry of some brave soul who probably saved the White House or Capitol Building. Innocence lost, the stark reality of evil regained in high-definition color.

But then there was that one that slammed into that one wing of the Pentagon. The one where Dad had been stationed.

I'd been attending classes at Georgetown University when it happened. The last day of a summer class I'd actually enjoyed.

Trigonometry. Go figure. We got word of the first two planes just after class began. At first we thought it was a tragic mistake, the one plane plowing into the one tower in a way that seemed super tragic but also super random. Like someone forgot to address a faulty indicator light during the pre-flight rundown, leading to mechanical failure and hella-crazy tragedy.

That theory went out the window when the second tower enveloped the second plane, that explosion of fire and glass on repeat for the rest of the day, smoke blooming from its wounded side. Right before the pair collapsed in a phantasmic show of fire and fury.

Classes got cancelled, which wasn't the worst thing in the world, and we were told to retire to our dorms to watch and process and grieve.

Then it happened. Swore I heard an echo of it all the way up the Potomac. Then a bloom of smoke all our own was seen spinning up into the sky. A smoke signal, not warning of danger but marking death.

In my case, the death of my dad.

So I did what any son would do: I signed up the minute I could to show those bastards back in Afghanistan who was boss, bleeding red, white, and blue all over that Army contract at the recruitment center. I was ready, willing, and able to avenge my father's death. Right after I graduated the next year. ROTC got me ready and got me in shape. Not that I was really out of shape. But playing quarterback for the Falls Church Jaguars senior year of high school was a whole other ball of wax compared to dropping and giving my drill sergeant eighty! Soon enough after graduating, I was at boot camp at Fort Benning, where I was tapped to join the Army Rangers before shipping out to that godforsaken land overseas in the heart of Operation Enduring Freedom. One thing led to another, and I was hunting down Donald Rumsfeld's deck of fifty-two of Iraq's most wanted.

Which was where I was now, lying in my bunk and trying to catch a wink of shut-eye after a sleepless night, sweat dripping down my face and soaking my Army-issued skivvies under a blanket of heat and humidity. The sun was breaking through the canvas now, and the sure-as-heck knowledge it was going to be one of those days, turning on a dime with heads-or-tails results that would have lasting repercussions, came ratcheting up my spine.

"Grey, on the double!" someone barked from the end of the cavernous canvas tent.

And not just Someone. *Major* Someone. The one with the power to send my ass into Saddam Hussein's palace if he wanted to.

Major Pepper. And boy was the man a lonely heart, with that bark and bite and bald head of his. But I was in his club, under his command. So I hopped out of the top bunk bed, on the double.

"Yes, sir," I yelled after I landed, back straight and legs snapped together. "Sergeant Grey reporting for duty."

"Well, put some clothes on then and meet me outside in thirty."

He turned to leave, and I had to ask: "Minutes, sir?"

There was a snorting snicker behind me before silence. Colton.

Pepper's boots scraped like sandpaper across the floor as he spun back around and strode over to me, getting in my face with that hot, humid, jalapeño breath of his.

"Thirty *SECONDS*, Grey!! And now *TWENTY!!* If I'da wanted you to take your sweet-ass time, I'da sent you to my Aunt Mildred to get your hair all gussied up, maybe do your nails and makeup, you sorry piece of crap enlisted nobody! Now get to it and meet me *OUTSIDE!!*"

I held my breath as the man left, the thin piece of plywood door slamming behind him with a weak whimper.

Then I hustled on the double to get into my fatigues as Colton razzed me for getting Major Pepper Breath on me for my wise-ass remark.

"Serves ya right, Silas," he said in that Texan drawl of his, the kid with a quarterback build sprawled out on his bed and flipping through some muscle car magazine his mom sent him in a care package. Must be nice. My mom died giving birth to me and my twin, Sebastian. And he had better things to do than send me care packages.

I yanked a sock down from my bed and threw it in his face as I zipped up my pants. He hollered and threw it back, the Army-issued white cotton lump sailing past my shoulder and hitting a new private sitting on his bed in the back of the head. We both laughed as I stuffed my T-shirt in my pants. Again, Army-issued, tan color 499.

"So whatcha think Major Pepper Breath wants with you?"

"Who the heck knows." I slouched into my camo shirt and whipped on my cap, then turned to leave—when Colton grabbed my arm. I turned around.

"Give him hell," he said with a grin.

I grinned back with a nod. "As always. But I gotta jet. Got like two seconds left before he rips me a new one!"

"Go West, young man!" he said as I trotted through the cheap excuse for a door. But it did the job, I guess, keeping out the sand and wind and riff raff.

But not the heat. It was as merciless outside as inside, the high-noon sun blinding on top of suffocating. An armored personnel carrier donning the same camo-pattern now clinging to my back in a sheet of sweat trundled by, the engine giving a grunting cough and its exhalations shaving seven years off my life. My slapdash barracks were part of Camp Liberty, one of the primo military installations in Baghdad since 2012 when Uncle Sam's finest took over the place. It was a sprawling place of concrete barriers and neatly lined pale beige buildings, some nothing more than the canvas monstrosities I lived in, making up our living quarters and offices and command-and-control centers, often as muddy as it was dry.

Glancing around, I spotted the Major huddled with a few others near a trio of M35 cargo trucks sandwiched between a pair of Humvees on either side. Looked like a decent-size mission with all the tonnage and pent-up firepower inside those mounted M2 machine guns and Mk 19 grenade launchers. So I hustled on the double over to his position, edging just in front of a platoon of grunts hoofing it in some cardio exercise at the hands of an even nastier Major Pain-in-the-Ass than Major Pepper Breath. Just happy I wasn't in that bunch.

Although, who knew what my CO had in store for me...

The man finished with the others as I walked up eyeing the beasts idling beside the Major, their back flaps pulled tight to hide their cargo—and their intent.

I whistled and said, "The Army must be in a world of hurt if it's still hauling these dinosaurs from my pop's generation. Thought we were looking forward to their replacement by the Light Medium Tactical Vehicle from some Austrian firm, not schlepping around in these bad boys from another war era."

"Watch your mouth, Grey," the man said with that Jersey accent coming through strong now—which meant I got his blood tweaked. Never a good thing, especially on a Monday.

Wiping a sheet of sweat running across his forehead, he added, "These bad boys from another war era, as you call them, are American-engineered dinosaurs. They've seen their fair share of combat over the decades defending your baby bottom and have come through to tell the tale. So show a little respect, would ya?"

I stiffened. "Yes, sir. Uh, you wanted to see me, sir?"

"I did. You've got a new assignment. You and your men."

I suppressed a grin, nodding at the man and taking pride in

another mission for my country. "Yes, sir. What would the Army have me to do?"

He yanked a thumb toward the M35s. "Commanding these bad boys from another war era into a town not far from here."

I knew my eyes widened with surprise, and I let slip a disappointed wheeze. But I quickly recovered with a nod.

Major Pepper chuckled. "Don't act so grateful, Sergeant. You're giving me heart palpitations with your exuberance."

I held a fist up to my mouth and cleared my throat. "Sorry, sir. It's just, well, what's the mission?"

He nodded toward the back end of one of the dinosaurs. "Go see for yourself."

I stepped over to the rear and hopped up on the bumper. Throwing back the dark canvas, I found an assortment of soccer balls stuffed in black netting. Black and white ones, neon green and orange ones, even rainbow balls. Had to have been forty or fifty of them.

I looked at Major Pepper, who was standing with arms folded, smirking at my confusion. I dismounted from the bumper and checked the other two. One was empty; the other was a replay of the same scene in the first truck: just packs of balls with some foodstuff thrown in for good measure.

Jumping down, I asked, "You want us to host a soccer tournament for the boys, Major? Break out the MREs and host a tailgate party in the middle of camp?"

"Not here. Back outside Mosul, Sergeant," the man grunted.

Which meant only one thing. We were heading back to continue what we'd started yesterday, where we'd handed out food and water and toys for the kids, and where that kid whooped my butt at soccer. One end of my mouth curled upward at the prospects of a rematch against that scrappy kid I'd sparred with for hours north of our position. I also didn't mind escaping not only the drudgery of camp but also harm's way by playing the part of humanitarian for Uncle Sam.

For the past few months since taking over their country, we'd been making progress trying to establish a U.S. presence in by befriending local Iraqi villages. Community relations, the Army called it. The day before, my men and I had handed out soccer balls to the kids in a village outside of Mosul. Even played a few matches with those balls. And boy, did those kids sure know how to play! Resurrecting my college passion and position, I played goalie, but it was no contest. We'd been bested for a five-to-two loss by a scrappy Iraqi boy half my age that I blamed on Colton.

The idea of going back to offer handouts to win over the hearts and minds of a country we'd basically given the finger to, even if it was in the interest of nation building—well, as much as I wanted that rematch, it sort of turned my stomach. By now, the prospects of finding Saddam's elusive WMDs were pretty dim, the whole reason we got into that mess in the first place. And now we were being ordered back to hand out fluorescent soccer balls and canned goods and bottles of water when what the Iraqi's really needed was their country back? Although I had to hand it to the good folks in that village: Even if they didn't understand the war, the villagers seemed to have appreciated our gesture. The kids sure did, anyway.

Didn't know what to make of it all, but orders were orders. So I said, "When do we leave?"

Major Pepper raised his wrist. "In thirty—"

My eyes widened, a replay of before springing me into action when I had to scramble on the double to get my clothes on.

"—*MINUTES*, Grey."

I slid to a halt, taking a breath and smiling before offering a chuckle. The Major slapped my back, and I took an off-kilter stumble forward before catching my footing and stiffening with respect.

"Geez, I'm not that much of a hard-ass, Grey. Get you

platoon together, then load up that beige military truck full of items intended to further appease the locals, while the politicians and nation-builders work toward putting the country back together again. *ON THE DOUBLE!*"

"Yes, sir!" I shouted, saluting my CO before beelining it back to the barracks.

One of those days, indeed…

I pushed through that blasted plywood door, finding Colton kneeling at another private's bed piled with two others playing a card game. Texas hold'em.

"Green!" I shouted to my right-hand man.

Colton jolted at the sound of his last name and spilled his cards on the bed. He cursed loudly, the fellas busting out laughing at him fumbling a flush.

I intercepted anything more, continuing: "Get the men ready to head out, on the double! Like the Major said earlier: *IN THIRTY—SECONDS!!*"

I left as the room scrambled to put themselves together. Happy to report that in twenty-eight seconds, every last one of my eighteen men were lined up outside, backs stiff and Colton strolling to meet me at the front of the line to make the twenty that was our platoon.

"You just had to go and ruin my bangin' hand, didn't ya?" he complained, slapping his cap on his shinny eight-ball head.

I suppressed a grin and explained the Major's orders. We were to load up and move back out to Mosul. He and I shared the desire for that rematch with those kids, as well as the chance to offer a hand of support to a people who were caught in the middle of geo-political nonsense that even we didn't fully understand. So we all got to it, on the double, shuffling across the dusty packed sand to load up and move out.

It was hot and sticky like most days, temperatures already pushing into the 90s. A slight breeze blew across the flat Iraqi grounds outside our military encampment, tinged with manure from the local pastures. I'd slept like crap the night before, but the thought of getting a rematch from the scrappy Iraqi teenager and his friends gave me enough energy to finish loading up the cases of shoes, medical supplies, and the rest of the foodstuff and water stacked next to the trucks that were meant to win the hearts and minds of their parents.

Finishing, the men moved out to their assigned vehicles: four to each of the big rigs, two up front and two poking their shiny new M4 carbine rifles out the back, while the other eight of us split into the two Humvees, Colton and me and two others taking the leading vehicle. In less than twenty minutes, we were trundling out between concrete barriers erected at the gate to Camp Liberty manned by more firepower than our Humvees and heading north toward destiny, kicking up a trail of beige dust in our wake and reaching for that rematch that we all needed after the year of hell we'd been through.

Inside the Humvee was worse than outside, Uncle Sam having the brilliant idea of outfitting the rigs with inch-thick armor and 3-inch thick windows that sealed off all relief to us troops inside. Rumor was that air conditioning was coming soon, but not soon enough. Felt like that sauna I'd frequented at Georgetown after soccer practice, letting the heat work out the sore from giving it all I had on the field. Except this was draining the energy from me, the hot suffocation compounded by the stench of us Rangers desperate for proper showers packed in like sardines. And after Colton let one rip, getting an earful from all three of us and darn-well near throwing his butt to the curb—let's just say I closed my eyes and dreamed of my happy place on an Alaskan cruise.

The trip was another rough one, the massive wheels of the Humvee hitting every pothole left in the wake of the shock-and-awe siege that had ravaged the land. Uncle Sam had rained down enough payloads to throw Iraq back to the Stone Age. And to be honest, they sort of did, leveling entire neighborhoods and airports and business districts in their quest to root out the Republican Guard and bring Saddam to his knees. Or in his case, crawling out of some rabbit hole on a farm in the middle of butt-freakin' nowhere.

And there we were, our four hours stretching to five before our eyes, even six, on our return trip thanks to another series of bombing raids and counterstrikes that had been the reason I'd slept like crap the night before.

"All I gotta say," Colton said, the pair of us in the rear two seats as two boys from some place called Kalamazoo, Michigan —wherever the heck that was—drove us onward, "when I get home, I'm booking a full-day of pampering at my neighborhood spa. Mani, pedi, a full-body massage, seaweed wrap with those burnin' hot stones they put on your back. The whole nine-yards after—"

The Humvee thumped with an especially wicked dip.

"—this."

I smirked. "All I gotta say, is that I'd hate to be the chick who has to pamper your sorry ass after what we've been through. Because I've seen those toes, and those things are nasty mother—"

Colton slugged me good in the shoulder. I laughed and put up my hands in surrender, backing off and taking in the view, which wasn't much of anything, mostly because not much of anything was left.

My grin faded into a frown taking in the despair, the landscape pockmarked by craters left by bombs lobbed by the Republican Guard as much as by Coalition Forces. And that wasn't even touching on the myriad of concrete buildings reduced to rubble and cars abandoned along the side of the road, some charred beyond recognition, and the huddled mass of tents with fires burning in barrels even at that hour and people wandering aimlessly—without work, without purpose, without hope.

Couldn't understand why humanity did this to themselves. Why God allowed it all, not intervening to bring all the war and chaos and injustice to a swift end. My Catholic upbringing taught me God worked all things for the good, and that the bad in the world is because of us humans using our free will for royally screwed-up ends. Seemed about right, but I couldn't quite wrap my mind around how a good God could allow so much bad in the world. Maybe that was why I had drifted so far from my childhood faith, abandoning the Church in college, a Catholic one at that, and seeking answers elsewhere. Maybe one day it would all make sense, something clicking in my head to reconcile the problem of evil—of human evil.

"Would you look at that..." Colton grumbled, gesturing toward the windshield. "Not even twenty minutes out and we've got ourselves an accident."

Which wasn't unusual in the slightest. Vehicles would often break down in the middle of the highways that ran through the desert countryside, either because of ill-repair or from running out of fuel. Even then, more were left as carcasses from the fallout of war. Felt like half the battle getting from one point to another was clearing away the automobile detritus to bring the godforsaken war to an end.

The traffic came to a crawl, rust buckets painted from across the muted rainbow spectrum in front and behind throwing up their disapproval. And there they were, three utility trucks sandwiched between Humvees stuck in the middle of butt-freakin' nowhere.

"Sergeant," my radio squawked at my side, a boxy thing that seemed like a holdover from Nam. It was Dan Williamson, point man in the rear Humvee. "What the hell is going on up there? We're riding blind back here, feeling like our pants are around our ankles."

You and me both, pal...

I leaned forward for a better viewing of the scene out front, snatching the radio without breaking my line of sight. It was no use. We were kissing the bumper of a big-ass delivery truck that had seen better days. Bread, by the look of it, which barely afforded the truck a tank of gas, let alone replacing the left rear shock that made it droop something fierce to one side.

Engaging the radio, I said, "Williamson, this is Grey. Roger that. Just keep our six from taking it up the backside by an RPG and sit tight. Over."

"Roger that, chief. Sitting tight and keeping your ass clear of foreign objects."

Colton laughed, as did the other two boys from Kalamazoo.

The truck lumbered forward, picking up speed as the traffic thinned, navigating whatever was up ahead and keeping their necks on straight. Hated rubberneckers, and Iraqis were the worst offenders. Although, he couldn't blame them, given what they'd been through. He'd probably look to see if he knew the poor soul stuck on the side of the road with all the chaos they'd witnessed.

Again, not unusual to come across an accident, and not unusual to get stopped along the way. Not preferred, but not unusual.

And yet...

This felt different. Didn't know why until something began needling the back of my lizard brain. Something deeply seated from ancestors battling mastodons and sabertooth tigers from eons ago in the interest of self-preservation. A sinking feeling began rising in my gut, and a cold dread began spreading through my veins.

The truck in front wound its way through the accident scene, and we followed several paces back, the others in the crew following close behind.

The whole thing gave me the heebie-jeebies. Didn't make sense why in the slightest at first glance, but it was how the cars were positioned. They were angled on both sides of the road, blocking passage in a way that seemed like the chaotic fallout from some sort of collision. And yet the closer we got, it seemed more staged than the end result of a chaos-theory based collision.

Almost like a barrier. Like they were meant to impede the flow of traffic.

Then I saw it before we reached it—but was too late to stop it.

On the left side of the Humvee. Nearly imperceptible for those who didn't have eyes to see.

And then we did. All of us.

A package at the backside of one of the cars, wires coming out all cattywampus, going this way and that.

Right before it exploded in a mushroom of fire and fury, destruction and death.

A bomb is a remarkable thing. Just latent force, bottled up all civil like until it's ready to be unleashed. At which point it's everywhere and nowhere at the same time, tearing and ripping and shredding and dismantling and consuming everything in reach—without discrimination.

Of course I saw it all unfold before I heard it. Just that split second that felt as if it was all happening at once.

Black smoke and the fires of hell itself bloomed outside our three-inch thick windows before it tore through the plating that was meant to shield our left flank with a roar and a thunderous explosion that all seemed to collide in some grand satanic symphony—at once blinding me and deafening me, the heat suffocating and blooming at my left side until we toppled over out of harm's way, being tossed like a rag doll onto the Iraqi highway shoulder.

Didn't know for sure, but figured the others behind had taken the same kind of heat, those black-and-white soccer balls and medical supplies and foodstuff meant to win over the hearts and minds of Iraq's countrymen clearly meaning jack squat now, given the sudden change in circumstances.

Nearly blacked out from it all, the force of the blast and the violent toppling and the acrid smoke flooding the cabin, but I held it together. A tuning-fork ting disoriented me, but it didn't stand in the way of regaining control of a mission that went to hell in an IED handbasket.

It was go time. Again.

I went to give an order until I looked down—and nearly lost it then and there.

I was still saddled in the toppled horse, my seat belt strapping me in. But draped over me was my right-hand man, my confidant.

My friend, my pal.

Colton Green.

Half of his body had landed on me, the left side blown clear off, from the arm down through his pelvis and legs, a mangled mess of intestines spilling out like bloated, slippery sausages, his flesh like ground beef.

Colton was crying, his eyes wide and flooded and searching for life, but clearly knowing little was left.

I reached for him, but pain lanced through my shoulder, something having been tweaked in toppling over. But adrenaline pushed me through, my arms going on autopilot to cradle the man who'd helped save my ass a time or two. The friend who'd helped me work through a sack full of my stuff left over from my dad dying and brother leaving me high and dry. The pal who'd beat me at hand after hand of Texas hold'em.

Moving my left arm, I pulled what was left of Colton toward me. He flopped down easily, the restraints that had held him firm giving way under the absence of any body to restrain.

"It's alright," I said with surprising resolve, voice steady and steely as I tried to reassure him. "You're going to be alright, Green. Just hold on a few more minutes!"

"Silas," he interrupted. "I need you to promise me something."

"Anything, buddy. Anything." Blood was spilling from him now, every crevice giving up his life force and his eyes nearly draining of it themselves.

"Silas, swear on the life of your future kids that you won't quit until every one of those terrorist bastards responsible for 9/11 are hunted down and gunned down."

Colton gasped for breath, blood gurgling out from his mouth and his eyes going wide.

Not much time left now.

I didn't know what to say, so I agreed, whispering: "I will, Colton. Mark my words, I'll kill every last one of those bastards..."

The man grinned, teeth stained crimson and face filled with delight right before coughing up another handful of blood.

I drew what was left of Colton in close, cradling the man as he breathed his last breaths.

"Everything's gonna be fine, you hear me, soldier?" I said through a thick throat and quivering lips. "Help is on the way. You stay with me, dammit!" I slapped his face and shook what little was left of his body, the shell of my former buddy like one of those dummies used for mouth-to-mouth resuscitation demonstrations.

That help eventually came, the rest of the platoon rushing over to drag us out from the fires of hell. But it was too late.

Colton was gone. For good.

It was the last memory I had of my wartime friend before I woke up in a hospital ward in Camp Liberty, bandaged and bruised but intact.

And alive.

The droning beeps and buzzes of monitors and IV dips in the bright, sanitized hospital ward were my only soundtrack.

White drapes lined both sides of me in my single cell clinging to rods above me, another curtain pulled at the foot of my bed. I ached, something fierce. Didn't know what time it was. What day it was. My head hurt, my back ached, my limbs were limp with exhaustion. Felt like I'd been run over by a truck. In some ways I had been, the force of the blast worth a thousand trucks rumbling over me.

But I was alive. And Colton...

The memory of all that blood and those slippery sausages spilling from the only half of his body made my head swim. I thought I'd retch, right then and there.

Heaving a desperate breath to stabilize my senses, I turned my head and saw something I didn't expect—resting on a stand next to my bed.

A Bible.

Didn't know who left it, or why. Didn't know if it was Army-issued or one of those Red Cross or Gideon religious organizations' doings. Regardless, anger welled up within me at the sight. At all it represented.

The Word of God. A God who was apparently too preoccupied with all the rest of the crap in the world than to give two rats' asses about two grunts on some backwoods highway in Iraq to prevent one of them from getting blown to smithereens!

I grabbed for it, my fingers clawing at its slick faux-leather cover. My face twisted up in revulsion so that I thought I really would retch now. I went to throw it through that damn curtain stained with the memory of countless other grunts who'd seen their own fair share of the face of sheer evil—when I stopped myself. Clenching it with white-knuckled anger and sadness and madness, I drew it to my chest.

Then I opened it, perhaps for the first time since childhood. Didn't pay much attention to where. Figured any place was as good as any when it came to the Good Book. What I stumbled on surprised me. Two words, popping off the page, the randomness of my search seizing my chest and constricting my throat with emotion and threatening my eyes with teary overload.

Jesus wept.

That's what it said.

Didn't make sense in the slightest, that the supposed Son of God would weep, would *need* to weep. I mean, he was God for God's sake! Yet there he was, crying.

I could relate.

So I flipped back to the start of the chapter, John 11, and started reading. Apparently, some guy named Lazarus was ill, and some of his friends went to tell Jesus he was on the verge of death, probably thinking he could work his magic and bring him back to health. But Jesus didn't go right away, and by the time he did it was too late.

When he finally arrived, Lazarus was already buried, going on four days. Reading between the lines, it was clear his friends weren't thrilled he hadn't answered their call for help. I could relate! But he said something to them that hit me upside the head.

'Your brother will rise again.'

I furrowed my brow, my Catholic catechism rising to the surface from years of neglect and understanding Jesus meant *the* resurrection. The belief that not only Jesus defeated death, but that we would as well through his power and glory. A line from the Nicene Creed quickly followed on the heels of that catechol reminder:

I believe in one, holy, catholic and apostolic Church. I confess one Baptism for the forgiveness of sins and I look forward to the resurrection of the dead and the life of the world to come. Amen.

"Amen..." I whispered, continuing to scan the bedside Bible when something else stopped me in my tracks:

Jesus said to her, "I am the resurrection and the life. Those who believe in me, even though they die, will live, and everyone who lives and believes in me will never die. Do you believe this?" She said to him, *"Yes, Lord, I believe that you are the Messiah, the Son of God, the one coming into the world."*

I closed the Bible now, recalling Colton making a similar confession and trying to talk to me about it. Didn't much care what he had to say, telling him I'd been raised in the faith and sort of left it behind. He didn't make a big deal about it, but he'd made a deal about Jesus' promise of new life after death.

Death. The great enemy. Of the world, but especially mine.

Mom had died giving birth to me and my brother, Sebastian. Dad had died at the hands of terrorist whack jobs. And now Colton.

I closed the Bible and set it back on the nightstand next to my bed, those blasted beeps of those blasted monitors continuing to drone on as I laid in my white-curtained cell. I folded my arms to consider this story from the Good Book.

There was Jesus, making a pretty ballsy promise that those who believed in him would rise again, defeating death with some cosmic middle finger.

And yet, there he was—weeping over the fact Lazarus had been laid in a tomb for four days.

Colton seemed to believe in Jesus; made that clear. Which I guess was the silver lining in the tragedy: Jesus' promise was Colton's promise.

But there was something else that quickly trailed that realization. Someone more powerful than the one that gave me hope that Colton was in the end alright.

Jesus himself wept at Colton's death.

I didn't know what to make of this story, but something in me broke at that realization. And I, Silas Grey, for the first time since burying Dad a few years ago in that grave in Arlington National Cemetery, followed Jesus' lead.

I wept.

For Colton and his family, for my men and what they had experienced on that fateful road. For me, and all the chaos of combat I'd witnessed up close and personal since 2002 when I was shipped overseas, and the best friend I'd lost far too soon, and all the emotion I'd kept in through sleepless nights with bombs dropping in the distance and men falling on my right and on my left.

And then I slept, having spent myself of all the bottled-up emotion while also resting in the twin truths that Jesus wept over Colton's death and Colton would live, would rise again.

Didn't make it easy. Just bearable.

Death sucks; I know that more than most. But something about Jesus weeping in its face made it a bit more bearable, knowing that the Son of God felt the same way I did after feeling its sting. And knowing he promised victory over it gave me a small measure of hope—for Colton, for my parents.

Sleep came quickly that day.

2. LAST TIME. PROMISE. (NAOMI TORRES)

Miami, Florida. The Magic City. A slice of paradise of white sand and even whiter coke, if you're into that sort of thing.

Me? Wasn't really the sort of gal who unfurled an umbrella and threw out a blanket to while away the day in Miami's white powder, preferring more adrenaline to my R&R. Certainly was never the sort of gal who snorted Miami's other white powder. Although...given what I've been through the past few years and the hot mess I was fixing to get into if I maintained my current trajectory in life—wouldn't be surprised if I ended up dipping into both powders at some point.

But this day would be the day I struck gold, I just knew it. Could feel it in my bones, as Papá would always say to Mamá when I was still a little *niñita* back in Mexico before things changed, convinced his fortunes would turn the corner.

He would come home after a long, grueling day's work at the car lot trying to convince men they should upgrade their ride for their marriage and family and prestige in the community. One would bite, another wouldn't, most would offer the well-worn excuse they needed to *'pensarlo'* overnight. Sometimes they would return after thinking it over; most would not.

So given the odds, you'd think Papá would have changed his tune rejection after rejection, or at least changed keys.

De ninguna manera!

I chuckled at the memory of the man who died far too young, knowing I inherited his stubbornness. Or perhaps stick-to-it-iveness. Either way. No way would Naomi Torres dream of changing tunes or changing keys or whatever when life handed me lemons. I'd hand it back a lemon meringue pie, mixing and matching new ingredients to bend life to my will.

Which I'd been doing since they died over twenty years ago, and then some more the past few years through grad school and an almost-marriage, and now after establishing myself professionally on the open market, and more on the black market. And yet...I needed a win. A big win.

And the dawn seemed to agree.

The morning air was warm and humid, tinged with salt and the expectant hope of a thousand potential dreams realized in the city of palm trees, fast cars, endless beaches, and even more endless parties stretching into the night.

The sun was peeking just above the horizon, waves gently lapping away from my crossed legs, the white sand I had grown to adore still cool from the night. A brown paper bag, mouth crumpled down, rested inside the bowl of my legs. I held a cup of hot black coffee, lid cast to the side and the heavenly scent of roasted beans wafting up my nose on an updraft of steam.

I closed my eyes and listened—the lapping waves joined by a pair of barking dogs and the deep grunt of some horn from some barge barreling through the Atlantic—then took a deep breath, my head filling with the scent of coffee and joined by the salty sea and *huevos rancheros* from some restaurant up the beach, before sipping the hot liquid and swallowing the nectar with a hum.

Heaven...

Only thing that would make my morning ritual complete was what lay inside the bag. With one hand I held my coffee while the other negotiated opening the bag, reaching for the soft, gooey goodness down inside.

A chocolate-covered yeast donut with a thick dollop of white frosting in the middle. A bird's nest, they called it. My favorite.

I snatched it and shoved it in my ready mouth, taking a bite and humming again with pleasure.

Nirvana...

Just chewing my chocolate donut with a nice lick of cream and sipping my surprisingly robust coffee, just listening to the waves lapping away a few feet beneath me, and thinking about all that had happened over the past year since moving out to join Tío with his company.

And all that I had left behind. Which amounted to *who* I'd left behind.

Grant Chrysostom. The one and only.

I wanted to hate the man after what he had done to me back in California while finishing my PhD. Leaving me as he did, engaged and planning a wedding, all because he had to "find himself." Wring his neck more like it! Imagine, me, Naomi Torres, being stood up so some SoCal beach bum could spend a year traveling South East Asian monasteries looking for tea that would make his world click into place?

I tore back into my bird's nest at the thought of it all, then washed down the fried dough and chocolate with a mouthful of brew, the brown nectar cooling enough for a larger swig.

He had found me! And then left me for himself, that's what he'd done.

But no matter. I was now the lead researcher at San Jose New World Salvage and Exploration, so eat that Grant!

Part historical and cultural preservation effort and part money-making venture, my uncle Juan from my father's side of the family started the gig after making most of his money exploiting oil drilling rights in Venezuela and Mexico. Tired of the corruption and boredom of that line of work, he took his earnings and put it to work trying to preserve his people's cultural heritage, while making a few pesos on the side. He hired me after I finished dual master's degrees in Mesoamerican and pre-Columbian studies at UCLA to lead the research team.

Another bite, another swig of coffee; another dog barking, another barge honking.

But it wasn't all bad. Tío had given me a good dose of responsibility, where in the last year I'd specialized in cataloguing the history of my people. Mostly the kind that sank to the seafloor in big wooden tubs flying flags from España four-hundred years ago, their wood having rotted away but their treasures there for the taking. Nothing major, just grunt work after the more seasoned veterans worked out in the field, but at least it was something.

For months, I'd been pestering Tío for my own gig, my own field to own. He's said my day will come, but I don't know. I mostly believe in my bones that he's right. But sometimes I feel like he's just patronizing me, the daughter of his brother and all. The doting uncle still taking care of his destitute *sobrina*.

But again, this morning was different. Something about getting up and sinking my toes in Miami's white sands, with this donut and this cup of coffee, with that dog barking and that barge honking and those *huevos rancheros* cooking in the backdrop—with all of it I could feel it in my bones that the moment would soon be mine.

Mine for the taking. For me and Tío, my Uncle Juan Manuel Torres.

A *purr-purr* interrupted my morning. My phone. I took another sip and set down my coffee in the sand, then reached for it.

Speaking of which…

I accepted the call and jostled the phone between my shoulder and head, picking back up my coffee and taking another bite.

"Hola, Tío! Buenos dias." I said between chews.

"Hola, Naomi, mi sobrina! Now, Naomi, what have I told you before? When in gringoland, speak as gringos, *bien?"*

I chuckled. The man had certainly acclimated to his new life in *El Norte*. But I guess so had I, thanks to his generosity with sending me to college and then to graduate school in the states. *Gracias a Dios* for Venezuelan oil money!

I took another bite and another sip. *"Sí, Tío. Que paso?"*

He huffed on the other. "I hear you're indulging in your favorite pastimes. Bird's nest, coffee, and beach, am I right?"

I chuckled again. Tío knew me well. *"Sí, sí."*

"Well, playtime's over. Back to the farm you go, *sobrina*. Today's the day."

I sat straight, sending coffee splashing on my legs. Thankfully it wasn't hot, and I barely noticed anyway. Did he say what I think he said?

I swallowed, holding my donut in one hand, my coffee in the other, and still cradling my phone.

"Sobrina…are you alive?" he asked.

"Sí—I mean, yes! I mean, what's this about?"

Now he chuckled, that deep, throaty laugh made husky by too many Cuban cigars. "Your first assignment. *Te veo pronto!"*

See you soon, is right!

I scarfed down the rest of my donut and drained my coffee, then dashed back to my car, tossing the empty Styrofoam cup in a trash can along the way.

What did I say? This day would be the day I struck gold. I'd known it. Could feel it in my bones!

Papá had taught me well.

Reaching my car, I didn't even bother opening the door. Just hopped inside my mustard yellow Passat convertible circa 1998, the year I graduated high school—a gift from Tío—and floored it, cutting off a man running in way-too-tight bicycle shorts but not caring a lick.

Because today was payday, in a big way!

Sound from the downtown emerging from its slumber filtered across the water, commuter cars and delivery trucks, combined with the gentle hum of boats and crashing waves and gulls cawing above. Part of the allure of Miami for me were the sounds, and this city had it all. I also loved its smells. The smell of fish and taste of salt on a gentle wind breezing off the water reminded me of the life I had here—with salvaging treasures under the sea and the promise of one day carefully peeling back layers of dirt to unearth forgotten civilizations.

I just prayed to *Dios* above that I didn't screw it up!

Heading south to an industrial district on the outskirts of Miami, I drove to a large warehouse near an inlet where a sizable expedition-style boat was docked. Seeing it made my heart skip a beat. I loved setting out on that fish with Burt and Maggie to uncover the mysteries of ancient cultures and salvaging those cultures for the world to enjoy. Could hardly believe my good fortune, that the man had not only adopted me after my parents passed away but that he had put me to work on his most important and ambitious business venture yet.

And now with my very first assignment, all on my own!

A three-story warehouse came into view behind a trio of massive elm trees dripping with Spanish moss, siding made of rusting corrugated metal and roof sagging under the weight of decades of neglect and seagull droppings. Crunching across the gravel parking lot, I pulled into a spot at the front, then turned off the car.

I sat still, unmoving, staring at the door to the facility I had walked through countless times, an entrance full of promise and expectation and purpose.

And now with my very first assignment, all on my own...

A sudden ping of doubt began worming its way through me. Could I really lead this team? Could I really find the sunken treasure that had eluded so many others? And when I did, could I keep myself from doing what I had done so many times before—insisting that *that* time would be the last time I snuck off some piece of history to sell to the highest bidder?

The minutes ticked by as I sat, sweating now from the rising sun baking my Passat, mulling over my future.

Then I took a breath, threw open my door, and slid out. "You've got this, Torres!"

Yeah, I did!

Didn't I?

Crunching toward the front entrance, I opened the door, finding no one around. Probably still at lunch. Then I heard laughter farther inside the space where we conducted our research and cataloged our finds. One voice rose above the rest, its familiar timbre comforting and welcoming. Uncle Juan.

I was nearly skipping now toward the sounds. I passed the break room, dark from lack of lighting and smelling like burnt coffee. I blamed Burt for that one; never could make a decent cup of Joe. An office with a large picture window greeted me, and a 70s-era steel executive desk inside with a lamp shining brightly on top was missing its captain. Tío's well-worn leather chair was turned away, a tear opening up on the seat back. Laughter floated my way again, urging me onward.

I made my way to the conference room with a low ceiling, cheap wood paneling covering the walls and more fluorescent lighting. A large table commanded the center, maps and documents strewn about, and a grouping of leather chairs and a couch sat at the other end.

I took a breath, lifted my chin, clinging to my self-belief that

I had this, and strolled into the room.

At once, the small group turned toward me. Maggie, a hard-scrabble woman with a head of long graying dark hair and an even longer history in treasure hunting and Tío's partner, was the first to see me. She acknowledged me with a knowing grin. Burt was next, the captain of the docked fish and director of operations who seemed equally pleased to see me. And then Tío, whose face was still shining with the punchline of the joke he had just told.

"There's my *sobrina*!" He opened his arms wide and walked toward me, a fat cigar sticking out of his mouth, and a drink of something caramel and alcoholic in one hand. Probably Cuban rum to go with his Cuban cigar.

I smiled and giggled. "What are we celebrating? It's just my first assignment. No biggie."

Burt grunted a chuckle, his generous belly jiggling under his stained white T-shirt. "No biggie? Oh, it's a biggie, alright!"

"But not because it's your first assignment, dear," Maggie reassured.

I furrowed my brow and looked at my uncle, shaking my head with wonder.

He took a puff of his cigar and then a drink before gesturing toward a group of leather chairs. "Come, come. Sit!"

I did, and he followed. The other two joined as well.

Another spicy, earthy cloud formed over the group with another long puff of Tío's cigar. He took another long swig of rum, then he got into it.

"Here is the deal," Tío said. "You will lead a team to a Spanish treasure fleet that went missing while returning from the New World to Spain in 1715."

My eyes went wide, my breath caught in my chest, my head felt faint at the lack of oxygen. Could hardly believe my ears, wondering if Tío really said what I thought he said—and meant.

The Urca de Lima...

After setting sail for the Old World on July 31, eleven of the twelve ships were lost in a hurricane near present-day Vero Beach, Florida. Also known as the 1715 Plate Fleet because it was carrying vast quantities of silver, the fleet had grabbed the imaginations of treasure hunters for a century. The crown jewel of the fleet was called the Urca de Lima for vast quantities of said silver.

"But, how? Why?" I swallowed hard. "Why me?"

Tío puffed another cloud of cigar smoke toward the ceiling and shrugged. "Why not? Besides, you've earned it with how hard you've worked the past year. As to the how." He sat forward and grinned widely. "We were approached by a wealthy businessman acting on behalf of the Cuban government to find the crown jewel of the fleet, the Urca de Lima."

"The Cuban government?"

He shrugged again and sat back, taking another swig of rum. "My business contacts from the past few decades seem to have served me well. Today we prep. A week from now we set sail. I am tasking you with handling the logistics and the recovery."

Another puff, another swig. "So, want the job?"

"Do I want the job?" I reached over and gave him a hug, pecking him on the cheek. I felt a bit embarrassed in front of Burt and Maggie, but I didn't care. "Thank you, Tío. Just...wow, thank you!"

"I'll take that as a yes!" Burt and Maggie laughed, so did I.

I nodded enthusiastically. "Yes, I'm in."

My uncle stood. "Then we get to work. And pronto! There is a lot to get done, because obviously we need to find the ship in order to secure the Cuban contract."

Now I stood, face falling with disappointment. "Wait, we don't have the contract yet?"

"First to verify the ship's location gets the gig," Burt

clarified.

"It's between us and three more outfits," Maggie added. "But they don't have a chance against us veterans and our newly minted researcher with two UCLA degrees!"

I looked at my uncle for some sort of reassurance, feeling the rug had been pulled from under me.

Tío shrugged. "Like I said, we need to move *muy rapido!*" He winked and slapped my shoulder. "So let's put our backs into it get to work!"

And work it was.

Over the next week, I spent every waking hour assembling meticulous research of past fleet records, eyewitness accounts, weather patterns. Even leveraged some newfangled LiDAR technology to assist in scoping out the Caribbean waters. Finally, I found, *we* found—because it was definitely a team effort—but San Jose New World Salvage and Exploration spotted the fleet in a deep-sea valley and became the proud owner of the contract from the Cuban government to explore every treasure hunter's and salvager's dream! That wasn't even touching on how discovering the sunken ship would catapult Tío's salvage company to the top-tier of Miami outfits.

And me...

The day we finally launched was perfect. Heaven, really. The sun was shining bright in a wide-open blue sky that portended even wider possibilities with a calm wind and relatively calm waves. Weather forecasted zero rain and the same conditions farther out near the sunken ship.

I was running late arriving to work, as usual, which didn't look so good as my first assignment. But Tío understood, saying the others had already begun to load the rig and get into position to retrieve history and make history.

After grabbing a donut and coffee, I scarfed down breakfast and parked at the warehouse, finishing my bites and the rest of the coffee before heading inside.

My pocket buzzed with an incoming text. I fished it out and checked it. My heart sinking.

Ozzy. My dealer I'd made buddy-buddy with to cash out on some of the smaller, more obscure trinkets I'd lifted from other salvages.

Heart picking up pace and breath following along, I swiped the phone to life to see what he had to say.

Hear you've scored the biggest fish of your career. Congrats! Ready, willing, and able to accept anything you want to unload. Hit me up. I'll be waiting. And expecting you.

Just great. Suppose I could be glad he was at least ready to deal. Then I'd be finished with the leach.

I promised myself that.

Last one. For sure.

It was fairly dead inside, which made sense since the others were already loaded up on the rig. Making my way through the warehouse past the breakroom and my uncle's office then into the main conference room, I headed into the garage out back where we catalogued our finds.

Every step through the cavernous space fired up all senses with delight. From the sight of the tables all arrayed, ready to receive history, to the smell of oil and gasoline, to the rattling of chains and lapping of the ocean through the open door at the end—not to mention the anticipation welling within setting sight on the sunken ship and dragging its remains to the surface. Perhaps take a few pieces and sell them on the side to my dealer. What a prize that would fetch!

I moved quietly through the dark garage lit by the full sun streaming through the open door at the end, a cavernous space that held deep-dive equipment, a LiDAR electronic imaging contraption, and a smaller boat with a rattly outboard motor I hated using. Glad Tío went with the larger diving support vessel, a massive thing painted red gleaming through the door. I smiled as I approached it, the waves lapping their welcomed rhythm and the distant city adding to the soundtrack. I approached the open door to the dock, its rough-hewn wood weathered from the decades.

When movement caught my attention a pace away.

I sucked in a startled breath and went to scream when I realized what it was.

A rat scurrying out of the door from the garage.

I cursed under my breath. Mostly cursing Tío. Lord knew I had complained from here to high heaven to him about the *regio ratas*. The Regal Rats, as I called them, since they seemed to have more say over the joint than my own uncle, scampering around like kings and queens, getting into this and that. It was an endless argument, but good-natured.

I let the fella go this time, then headed out, when a voice behind called after me.

"Ms. Torres, is that right?"

I didn't recognize it, but it was deep and buttery and lilting with a recognizable Spanish accent, more Caribbean than anything.

A well-appointed man in a tan suite, light blue shirt, pink and green patterned tie with matching pocket square approached, hand extended. "Raphael Pireto," he said, "a representative with *Ministerio de Cultura del Gobierno Cubano*."

I took in a measured breath and swallowed. The Cuban government sent over a representative of their Ministry of Culture. Just great. Someone else to deal with.

I put on my best smile and shook his hand. "Pleasure, señor Pireto."

The man laughed, hair black and slicked back with style. "Raphael is fine. We are so pleased with your work so far, I just had to see it for myself!"

You mean spy for yourself...

"Are we ready to set sail?"

I chuckled. "We?"

"Yes, I am joining you for the jaunt. To help catalogue the finds and report back to my very grateful government on all that you are helping us achieve, with retrieving our cultural heritage and history."

Yep. Came to spy. But what could I do? So I welcomed him and led the way to the boat that looked like it was ready to go.

The ride over was a jubilant affair, everyone ready to bring in the largest haul of our careers. With little wind and wave resistance, we skated across the water to the site and began, the divers plunging in to begin the delicate work of hauling up to the surface from the depths below the treasures left behind by history.

Seemed to take a lifetime, but soon the first of the treasures were pulled aboard with an elaborate pulley and cage, the fenced-in box stuffed with wood chests and gold and silver candelabras and other pieces in gold I couldn't identify right away, but that could wait. What mattered was that we'd hit pay dirt!

And then we'd see if I could get some more out of it all on the side.

We worked through the morning, through lunch with a few snacks here and there, and through the afternoon, bringing in cage after cage of more chests full of gold and silver coins, gold and silver figurines, more gold and silver candelabras— anything and everything else that had survived their watery grave and the test of time. When the ship was filled and the crew was spent, we went back to unload and rest up for the night until another day of hauling.

All of us were running on adrenaline by the time we made it back to shore. Tío had called ahead to have a dozen pizzas delivered. Seemed like overkill, a pizza a person, but we were entirely famished, and the food gave us fuel to unload it all and arrange the pieces on the tables dotting the garage.

By the end of the night, the crew was spent, everyone

filtering out to get rest for another day tomorrow, repeating it all in the morning. Even Tío was exhausted from it all, mostly from smoking and drinking while we did the real work, but he'd earned his keep.

"Well done, *sobrina*," he said, patting me on the shoulder before he left. "Your first assignment went without a hitch!"

I chuckled. "So far. But we've got a week of this, so you never know what tomorrow will bring!"

He kissed me on the cheek. "I knew you could do it. I knew you'd be great."

I smiled, pushing a stray lock of hair behind my ear. "Thanks. I'll stay and shut down the joint. I want to catalogue a few things before leaving."

"Always the workhorse, you are. Take after your tío! Don't stay too long!" He turned and left. Then he added with a shout: "I'm so proud of you!"

I watched him leave, a pit growing in my stomach at what I was about to do. It wasn't that I had to catalogue anything. It's what I had seen that I wanted to sell. Some coins no one would miss. A few of the tens of candelabras no one had noticed. Then a music box and a few combs. More elaborate than anything I had sold before. And expensive—and lucrative.

But first, to see if Ozzy was interested. I pulled out my phone and texted the usual: *'Looking for a good time?'*

That way, if anyone was listening in, they'd think we were doing something far different from swapping stolen cultural artifacts for payment.

Didn't take long until he replied, *'Let me know when you're good and ready ;)'*

The deal was set.

Time to get to work.

Last time. Promise.

After I was sure no one else was around, I got to work.

Snatching the candelabras I had spotted earlier, I made my

way back through the conference room, through the hallway, back outside and to my car, stuffing the pieces under my passenger seat.

Then I repeated it all in reverse, moving fast back into the garage for the music box and the five combs. I stuffed those in my back pocket and held the box against my chest, then weaved back through the tables and into the conference room on my way through the hallway and out the front door.

I opened my driver's door slowly, knowing the thing creaked to high heaven. It gave a whimpering cry, but I could live with it. I stuffed the contraband under my front seat.

Now a final trip. Grabbing the coins, I stuffed them in my pockets in a panic, more than I intended but didn't have time to feel bad about it.

I repeated the pattern: garage to the conference room, then hallway to the front and my car, where I planned to drop the coins in my center console.

Fishing them out of my pocket, a few clattered to the gravel in my clumsy nervousness. I spun around, the sound feeling like pots and pans banging away in the silent midnight air.

Holding my breath, I waited, but no one was around.

I gathered them from the ground and scrambled inside my car, slipping them inside their temporary home.

I was dripping with sweat now, even though the sun had set long ago and a cool breeze had washed inland from the ocean. I pushed my hair back and took a breath as I weaved back through the maze of my uncle's warehouse. After shutting off the lights to the garage, I texted Ozzy: *'Meet me at the usual location.'*

He texted back. *'Roger, roger. See you soon.'*

I closed my eyes then slid the phone in my pocket.

Last time.

Promise!

Throwing on my phone light, I hit the office lights one by

one on my way out. Locked the front door tight and crunched across the gravel lot.

I threw open my car door, not caring at this point what sound it made. Time to leave. It screamed, but I slid in and shut it fast. I fumbled with my keys to start the car, a few false starts getting the key in the ignition but finally succeeding. It roared to life and soon I was kicking up stones behind my car on my way to the dock.

For the final time.

Definitely promise...

"This is so incredibly stupid..." I muttered to myself, the wind whipping my hair around from the open windows of my car as I raced to meet Ozzy.

I slowed, fearing a police car would catch me speeding and pull me over. Soon I was arriving at an old abandoned wharf where a single silver Mercedes was waiting.

I pulled up next to it, the nightlife out in those parts on the outskirts of town chirping away in a deafening roar of wildlife. He stepped out, putting away a cigarette as I parked.

"My fav *mamacita*!" Ozzy said. "How are you?"

"Keep your voice down, will you?" I complained through my open window.

Putting the car in *'Park,'* I hopped out and started unloading.

"Help me with this, will you?"

"No pillow talk tonight, I guess," he complained before taking the music box and combs. He whistled as he set them in his open trunk while I got the coins. "Some fine thievery this time around, Bonnie."

That was the name I'd given the man. I didn't respond, unloading the coins in his trunk myself, ready to be done with it all. I returned to my car and grabbed the candelabras, handing them off to Ozzy.

"No one finds out about this, right?" I asked as he tossed them in his trunk and slammed the lid.

The man's gold tooth glinted in the brake lights from behind a wide grin. "Who do you take me for, *mamacita?* Always on the DL, you know that."

"Yeah, right, I know that."

He tossed me a wad of hundred-dollar bills rubber-banded together. I caught it with one hand. Far more than I'd ever gotten before! Looked like drug money from some dealer, which sort of fit.

I flipped through the cash, counting it. More money than I could have dreamed of, a weak smile playing across my face.

But that was it. Done for good.

"Last time. Promise..." I mumbled to myself.

"What was that?" he asked.

I shoved it in my pocket. "Thanks, Ozzy. For everything. I'll be seeing you."

Not...

Then I walked away, went back to my car, and drove back to my apartment in silence. It had been a long day, a bittersweet day, but a long one. I'd just overseen the largest find of any salvager in decades. I'd done a good job too, without any issues. And then I'd sold part of it for a year salary. For the last time, yes, but without any issues, without even thinking about it.

I'd hated what I'd become. The lying and stealing. But the thrill of it all and the high—man, was it hard to let go.

This time was the last time, though.

"Promise..." I muttered again, throwing off my shoes. I went straight to bed and drifted into dreamland without a problem.

Sleep came hard and fast; it was rudely interrupted by a loud pounding at my apartment door.

There was a pinkish glow through the curtains pulled at the large picture window of my living room, so it was still early morning.

Who in the world—

Another hard *rap-rap*, followed by an even harder *pound-pound-pound*.

The time on the microwave said 6:23, so it wasn't Tío because I wasn't due in for another hour.

Probably the landlord. Rent was past due by a week. But thanks to the little black-market swap of a few doubloons, that was gonna change.

I looked through the peephole, recoiling in confusion.

"Que es esto..."

"Ms. Torres!" a muffled voice sounded through the door. "Open up!"

A cold dread swept over me from head to toe. A well-worn trope of trashy bargain-bin ebook thrillers, but that's exactly how it felt. The adrenaline rush spread from my brain to my bowels, making both watery.

I swallowed hard, wondering why uniformed men with yellow *'FBI'* letters set against their dark chests. were banging away at my door. But also knowing deep down what it was all about.

I'd been caught.

Finally.

Part of me was grateful. Would let me live in freedom again, out from under hiding's shadow. However that looked after the FBI got through with me.

Taking a breath, I opened the door—walking through the portal to what came next.

"Ms. Torres?" said the tall, wide man with trimmed blond hair wearing a navy suit, angular face hard but blue eyes more warm than ice cold.

I swallowed hard. "Yes, I am her."

He pulled out a badge and held it up. "My name is Agent Keener. I'm with the FBI here to serve a warrant for your arrest in conjunction with INTERPOL."

There it was; that confirmed it.

The International Criminal Police Organization. The kind of international criminal police organization that investigated and prosecuted theft of cultural objects from world heritage sites.

"Would you come with us, please?" the agent said.

I sighed, as if releasing the weight of all that I had done in that single breath. Then I smiled and nodded, and off we went.

It was a quiet and quick drive in the back of a black government Suburban that screamed cliché. The men drove me to the FBI's Miami field office. It parked in a lot behind a sprawling complex of glass and steel that looked like something out of a Salvador Dali painting. Turned my stomach looking at the thing, mostly because I knew what it meant. For me, for Tío...

Didn't take long, and she was booked and brought into a cramped room painted white with a small table, two chairs on either side, and a mirrored window.

I took a seat and Keener sat across from me with a female agent who introduced herself as Cohick standing at the back.

Keener did the talking. "You're in some trouble, little missy. You see, we've been watching you for a while now after INTERPOL alerted us to some inconsistent reporting from your uncle's business dealings. I'll cut right to the chase." He slammed a thick file on the table, and continued, "We have hard evidence you have been stealing precious artifacts from the salvages you have been working, a one Ozzy Quintana acting as an informant for our little operation."

My heart sank. It was all a setup from the start.

"What we can't understand is, were you the brains of this operation or your uncle? And who else was involved up the food chain of this major operation?"

My eyes went large; my bowels went watery. No way was my uncle getting pegged for something I had done!

I stood. "No! Tío had nothing to do with this! I swear..."

Cohick stepped forward; Keener remained seated. She shouted, "Sit down! Another outburst and we'll cuff you to the chair."

I swallowed hard and obeyed, settling in for what I expected was going to be a long day.

"If not your uncle," Keener continued, "then give it to us straight. And remember, we've got plenty of details on you, little missy."

I pushed a lock of hair behind my ears, ready to confess. "It had started innocently enough. A few small pieces here and there from the collections I'd discovered. The coins and figurines and pottery were worth hardly anything to anybody anyway."

"So you figured," Keener said, "with all the business you'd been providing your uncle with your reputation and expertise, you figured he owed you. Is that right?"

I hung my head and nodded, saying nothing more.

"And?"

I looked at him. "And, that was it. I made a return trip to the Urca de Lima cache and took some of the more elaborate gold pieces, thinking I could double my earnings."

"So it was all about the money then," the woman at the back asked.

Again, I hung my head and nodded, saying nothing.

"Let me tell you what your first mistake was, sweetheart," Keener began. The way the *gringo* said it like that—*sweetheart* —like some two-bit cowboy made my blood boil. "Your first mistake was taking them in the first place. Especially since it had been a government-sponsored salvage. Cubans don't particularly like being taken advantage of."

It was true. It was also understandable, given uncovering the sizable Spanish fleet had been a boon for the Cuban culture, not to mention the economy and political climate. And their attention to the site was more than I had expected.

"Your second mistake was trying to sell the items on the black market. I mean, come on! What were you thinking, sweetheart?"

I still couldn't say, couldn't answer the obvious question. *Why?* Other than bald-faced greed, I couldn't say why I had betrayed my cultural heritage by trying to sell to the highest bidder.

"So if your uncle isn't involved, as you suggest, then who else?"

I shrugged. "No one. It was just me."

Keener slammed his hand down on the table. "Liar!"

"I swear! I was the only one involved. It was all me."

Cohick said, "No way you get away with this and it only be you."

I chuckled and shook my head. "Sorry. The INTERPOL sting certainly accomplished what you set out to do. Caught me red-handed. Too bad you thought you caught a whale-shark dealer when in reality you caught a minnow-of-a-researcher who had made a terrible choice."

Keener leaned back and fixed me with a searching gaze. "Bull."

I stared back, leaning forward and placing both hands on the table. "I'm tell you the truth. It was me. Not my uncle, not Burt and Maggie, not anyone else."

The man looked back at his partner, who hadn't said anything for a while. She shrugged and he turned back around, saying nothing for the longest time, the two of us staring one another down.

Finally, the man spoke: "Alright, if that's how you're going to play this. Although, for some reason, I believe you. Unfortunate, but I believe you." He stood, the chair sliding across the linoleum floor like nails on a chalkboard, then walked to the door. "Sit tight, sweetheart. I'll be back later, but you've got no one left but me looking out for you. So you think long and hard about how you're going to help me help you get out of this mess."

He left, locking the door behind him.

And sit tight I did. For hours, in that chair, at the table, pacing around the room. Thinking about what I had done, the decisions, the choices weighing on me.

The greed.

The betrayal.

Keener was right: I thought I was owed more. Even after all that Tío had done for me! I could have ended up in some black hole in the Mexican child welfare system, which really wasn't at all a system but more a prison for society's discards. Or in my case, those left behind from dead parents.

My heart was pounding, my head was aching, my chest was constricting in on itself from the weight of it all, searching and seeking breath, more breath to keep me alive under the weight of the realization. Except I didn't want any more breath, didn't want to live after what I had done.

To live with myself after how I had betrayed my uncle.

Thought I was having a heart attack with how I felt. Nope, just hyperventilating from it all. Had learned to tell the difference between the two after the first time it had happened back in Mexico after Papa's and Mama's death. Then again when Grant left. And now, there I was, in an FBI holding cell at the request of INTERPOL, the Cuban government even.

I stopped pacing at a corner of the room and slid to my bottom, my eyes welling with tears now and throat constricting with emotion until it all came out, my head between my legs and my body heaving and wracking from sorrow.

Didn't know how long it went on like this until the door shuddered and opened, startling me to attention.

I stood, Keener walking in with a smirk on his face.

"Looks like you've still got someone more than me looking out for you. Come on. You're free to go."

Hope rose within me, to the point I even allowed myself to smile, as faint as it was.

Tío!

Keener guided me over to a counter where he processed me out, then he showed me the door where he said my ride out of the joint was waiting.

As apprehensive as I was, not feeling like I could face the man who had saved my life, only to betray him in such a way, I figured if he came for me then all was not as bad as I thought.

Signing my name and collecting my things, I pushed through the metal door leading out into the lobby, ready to confess it all to my uncle and try to repair the relationship I had severed.

But he wasn't there. Instead Burt, all six-foot-five and nearly three-hundred pounds of him, was standing in his dirty T-shirt with hands in the pockets to his dirty blue jeans.

I looked around the glass vestibule, expecting my uncle to come out from the men's room or from some corridor after taking a phone call, but there was no one else.

Only Burt.

"Come on, kid. Let's get you home."

We drove in silence in his blue Ford F-150 from a few decades back. Out past the glass Salvador Dali building, through downtown Miami, along the coast, and toward the industrial park that held Tío's warehouse. Burt wasn't much of a talker, anyhow, but there was also not much to say. I'd screwed up. He knew it, and it was only then that I realized it affected him and Maggie, as well, not just my uncle. Their jobs and livelihoods were on the line just as much as his.

Before he parked, I asked, "H—How did I get out?"

Burt threw the Ford into '*Park*.' "Your uncle stepped in and got the Cuban government to drop the charges."

It had been hours, half a day since I had been picked up and brought to the field office, then several more as I was interrogated and was left waiting in that room. My uncle must have spent every hour trying to bend Cuba to his will. If anyone could, it was Tío, but I knew it would come at a price.

A large one.

Burt sat still and nodded toward the door at the warehouse. "He's waiting for you inside," was all he said.

I took a breath and nodded myself, getting out and going inside.

It was dark and quiet, the soft hint of spice and earth wafting my way from deep inside the building. Tío was probably smoking a cigar, which meant he was also drinking rum. The two went together with him, and he only did both when he was celebrating or mourning.

It didn't take a genius to know which was which.

My stomach clenched with dread the farther I walked inside, taking careful steps toward the back, every room dark, lights off. Even the conference room at the end of the hallway was vacant of life, the only light slicing into the windowless darkness from the open door leading out into the garage, where the spicy and earthy smoke was more pronounced.

Swallowing hard, I went inside, the cavernous garage cleared of the boat that had been trailered before. In the middle was Tío, a gray cloud hovering above.

"You know..." he started, a faint orange glow blooming from the end of his mouth, the cigar he was puffing, his back angled toward me.

The suddenness of his words in the stillness of the darkened space startled me, his deep, silky voice echoing throughout the vast space. Must have heard me come in. Or sensed my presence; he always had a way of doing that from when I was a teenager.

"I had always wanted to be an archaeologist. Like Indiana Jones, I suppose, although he was way past my time. Loved the sense of adventure, loved the idea of retrieving the past. Much like you, actually. Things turned out differently for me, for a number of reasons. But with you...I thought that I could provide for you what I could not do myself."

Another puff, that orange glow offering a silent rebuke in the silent darkness.

"And then this..."

This.

That was all. Undefined, and yet saying it all.

I walked toward him, not wanting to engage this way with such a gulf between us, stopping a few feet away.

"Tío..." I started, my hands held in front of me and wringing themselves into knots with nervous, anxious energy. "I am so, so sorry."

Tío turned around, his head bowed. He said through gritted teeth, "The Cuban government fined me and the company, given that we were the custodians of the excavation. They have severed their relationship with us. I imagine this will have a rippling effect across all of my other business relationships. Thankfully, I've been able to hold onto those contracts. But—"

He seemed to take a breath, but I realized he was choking back emotion. He continued, "But not before the damage has been done to *mi reputación.*"

My mouth opened for a reply, but none came. There were no words; there wasn't even any air for them. I felt sucker-punched in the gut, all air leaving me at the revelations.

"*Como pudiste...*" Tío said on a shaking breath, usually only reverting to his mother tongue when he was pissed. Right before he screamed: "*HOW COULD YOU?!?*"

I was thrown by his rage, literally taking a step back. Never in all my life had I seen him get so angry. Not even when he was betrayed by business partners in Venezuela. Hurt, yes, and angry. But not enraged. Not spittle flying from his mouth and face reddening and eyes bulging; not what little hair he had left standing on edge and that corkscrew vein of his popping at the side of his temple; not his teeth baring so that I thought he would tear my flesh right off my bone, then and there.

Again, my mouth fell open—more from shock than anything, but also for those elusive words.

"Tío…" was the only thing I could manage.

He put out a finger. "No! Do NOT *Tío* me. Answer me this: How could you do such a thing, after all I did for you? Taking you in as a teenager when your parents were killed by that damn drunk driver? I treated you like *mi familia, sobrina*. No," he said, closing his eyes and shaking his head before hanging it low. "You *were* family, as if you were my own flesh and blood. And this is how you repay me? By taking away my business, my livelihood, *MI VIDA?*"

Another sucker-punch to the gut. But he was right. I was family. Which made the betrayal all the worse.

He threw back the rest of his drink and bowed his head, then turned his back to me and headed for the door. "Get out…"

"Tío…" Again, the only thing I could manage.

The man spun back toward me. *"SAL!!!"*

Again, face reddened and eyes bulging and hair standing on edge. Same for the corkscrew vein popping at the side of his temple and teeth baring with lips pulled back.

Now he pulled back his glass as if he was about to throw it at me. I was instantly shaken at the sight, the threatening gesture. A shudder visibly ran through my entire body, which seemed to snap him out of it.

He himself startled, relaxing some and looking at his hand. He heaved a breath and sighed, then closed his eyes and dropped the glass to the floor with a shatter.

"Go, Naomi."

Naomi…

Not *mi sobrina*?

He looked at me, eyes blank and face fallen. "And in case it wasn't clear: *Estas despedida!*"

Fired. There it was.

Then Tío sent spittle flying to the cold concrete floor and walked out the door leading to the dock.

Leaving me.

For good.

I drove back to my apartment in silence; nothing to say, no one to say it to anyway. I went inside and shut the front door. I meant to go to my bedroom, to collapse into bed and sleep my life away, wishing dreamland would envelope me. Hoped either this had all been a nightmare, and I'd wake up, or I would fade away.

Because I had no idea what was next for me, what was *left* for me.

But I didn't; I couldn't. I stood still, like petrified wood. Immobile.

I looked around at what I had. Which basically amounted to nothing. I'd thrown it away, and for what? The thrill and high from stealing? What a waste.

I collapsed to my knees, then onto my side, lying on the floor. Still saying nothing, still shedding not a tear.

But then something happened. Something I hadn't done in twenty years.

For the first time since my parents died, I said a prayer.

For forgiveness, mostly, but also for help.

Would it matter; would it make a difference?

I wasn't sure.

Somehow I remembered my Abuelo priest saying the Lord promised he would never leave us nor forsake us, his children.

So I put that promise to a test, all night long.

It seemed like the first place to start.

Tomorrow? Who knew. I prayed it would take care of itself.

Because I had sure made a mess of today.

And tomorrow was all I had left.

 **THE VOICE AND THE NAME
(CELESTE BOURNE)**

"Bye, Mum!" I shouted from the threshold of the door to our dodgy home in North London. Nearly closed the door before mum shouted back.

Then I heard the whispering echo of her bunny slippers trundling down the stairs to our maisonette, a dreadful two-story eyesore of a flat built nearly a century ago.

Suppose I should be grateful, as it afforded me my very own room, but I was always pestering Daddy about upgrading to something more fashionable, given the house my mate lived in, daughter of a surgeon and all.

Speaking of which, I raised my wrist and checked the time. Drats. Running late again. She would bite my head off if I didn't get moving. But Mum had her way about her, and I knew what was coming. So I kept going, easing the door shut when I heard it loud and clear.

"Celeste, dear!" she called after me, with that shrilly voice in that perfectly posh Queen's English that stood my teeth on edge. I understood perfectly enough that she was bred for the part, having been boarded at Cobham Hall and readied for a very different life than she had chosen. But it still set my teeth on edge.

She was also loud enough I could not simply shut the door the rest of the way and pretend I hadn't heard her. Mum's pace picked up steam as I continued with the door. I closed my eyes, took a breath, then took a pause before opening it back up with a smile.

"Yes, Mum? Running late and—"

"As usual," she said, lowering her chin and raising a brow.

I hated when she did that. And I hated when she pointed out my character flaws. Especially running late, which had become something of a running joke in the family. My grin sagged, but I stiffened it and straightened.

"Yes, Mum. But surely you wouldn't want me to keep Hannah waiting."

"Of course not, dear. I only wanted to wish Maggie Thatcher a good night off!"

I giggled, strutting my hips to the side and putting a hand under my hair swept up tightly against my head in the late Prime Minister's immaculate bouffant style. Only mine was darker than the leading lady's blond, which was fine. Tried dying it to match but turned out a horrid mixture of colors that looked closer to cinnamon sugar quick bread than the hairstyle to my Halloween costume.

Mum returned the giggle and wrapped her arms around me. She held me, saying, "My little pumpkin, all grown. Sporting Margaret's best, too. Charcoal skirt, and pearls, and all!"

"But of course, Mum. Must carry on the Iron Lady's trademark attire!"

She leaned back and folded her arms, a smile continuing to play across her face. "Can hardly believe this is the last of your trick-or-treating. And to think, the holiday was just starting to gain steam here in the British Isles, no thanks to those Yanks across the pond."

"Guy Fawkes Day just doesn't have the same appeal, I suppose."

Mum laughed. "I suppose not. Just be safe." She stuck her finger out and put on her best parental face, adding: "And more importantly, have fun. Only a few months left to be a kid until adulthood is foist upon you."

"I will, Mum. Promise." I crossed my heart and giggled, thinking Mum wasn't so bad after all. Although, she didn't know the full measure of it...

"Good girl." She stood smiling while we held hands. "So, are Hannah's parents going to be around?"

I scoffed and sighed. "Mum..." Then I turned to leave.

She yanked me back. "What? Just asking. After all, I'm still your mum for a little while longer."

I gave her those eyes she had known for seventeen years, communicating annoyance but also appreciation for caring enough to keep me safe. After all, she was still my mum for a little while longer.

"Both parents will be present, if you must know."

She threw up her hands in surrender. She gave me one more snuggly hug before wishing me well.

"Jolly good. Carry on, then. And bob an apple or two for me, won't you?"

"Will do!" I said, dashing out the door before she could harangue me some more.

Hannah lived in a three-story terraced house several blocks away in a posher side of North London. Funny how that works, the dividing lines between the well-off and the middle-classers such as my parents, who were professionals in their own right but not of the surgeon class, but still. Such demarcations never dawned on me until I aged further along. Even at our all-girls preparatory school, with the mandatory uniforms and bans on jewelry, we all knew the food chain. And where we fell.

But Hannah was different. Didn't let the fact her father was one of the foremost surgeons in London—who employed a staff of help at their home and cruised the streets in a Lamborghini Diablo to and from work—get in the way of our friendship. Our ratty Peugeot seemed to always be on its last leg, and Mum took the Tube anyway to work and back. Didn't much matter to my mate, who opened up her arms wide to anyone in need.

Not that that was me. That I was in need of her charity or something. She was just an open person, far more open than I. Yet her invitation meant everything. The world, really.

I couldn't figure what she was playing at, though, with her going on about the secretive nature of the party and all. Figured it had something to do with the last time I'd spent the night, which had given me the creeps up and down! I hoped it wasn't a repeat of *that* night, given what had happened...

Either way, I was just happy to be out from under the watchful eye of my parents! And I had heard Thomas was going to be at the party anyhow. Which was all the more reason to be excited!

I sighed, breathing in the leaves strewn about the footpath through my neighborhood, the heady scent of earth and decay heaving in the air. Which made me have a think about, of all things, *class*.

Class, class, class, class. That's all anyone ever went on about. Or at least my parents.

Never understood why and what they were playing at, given that their roles in the British economic and cultural spheres put them in a class of their own. Daddy was a writer with several novels under his belt; Mum a publisher with one of the leading publishing houses in the country. A match made in heaven, really. A bit too perfect, but they got along alright, especially compared to my school mates whose parents were splitting left and right. Even at seventeen, I understood we had all the trappings that plenty of pounds could buy. Descent house, nice clothes, plenty of food from across the British Empire, what was left of it anyway. But it never seemed to be enough for them.

But enough of that; enough of them. I had better things to think about.

It was my final year of secondary school, and I wanted a night of frolicking with my mates, much to the dismay of Mum. It was Halloween, and I was set to celebrate later on at a bonfire with all my mates from school. One of the last flings of our cohort before we shoved off to our various adventures. Oxford for me, Manchester for Hannah, Cambridge for the Drake twins. Then there was Thomas, who was staying behind with visions of making it as a playwright, or at least making it big on the stages of London's finest theaters.

I found myself grinning; couldn't help it. The scent of his cologne lay heavy on the blouse I was wearing the last time he and I snogged in the broom closet at school. Grapefruit and coriander. That, combined with the continued rot of fallen leaves and the distant smoke of burning wood, the sun now cresting beneath the horizon and setting it aflame, and sent my head spinning into the stratosphere with desire. Golly, I loved autumn!

And I loved parties, and this one promised to be a right smashing good time, if Hannah had anything to say about it! Dressing as Prime Minister Thatcher should have put Mum at ease. But I understood the company I kept gave her a continued fright. I also understood it was probably a bit more than that, my parents having a chat with me recently about my religious direction.

It was quite the conversation, given I hadn't grown up in the Church. Given neither Mum nor Daddy brought me up in the Church, or at least a proper church. My parents preferred their Christianity to be personal and freelance more than religious and institutional. I wasn't very grounded in my faith. Which is what probably transpired in what Mum had termed my "dark phase" of late.

I thought she'd gone positively mad! As if I was stalking my school hallways in charcoal leggings and black cardigan sweaters, painting my nails eggplant and spritzing dark and brooding fragrances. Nothing could have been further from the truth of it, much more preferring frilly, girly attire than what the goths donned!

And yet...that also wasn't the entire truth of it, knowing my shadow side began piquing my interest more than the light of Christ. It had all started innocently enough, with a Ouija board during a sleepover at Hannah's house.

A wind picked up its pace from behind, dried leaves blowing past and the scent of burning wood gusting along with it. I pulled my coat tighter and kept my arms wrapped around my body for heat, my mind pulsing with memory from that fateful night.

A perfectly coined cliché, I know. Straight out of some supermarket rag, it is. But that's the truth of it. The board was a vintage thing made of honey wood with black lettering and numbers branded into it, smelling of mothballs and a musty basement. Apparently, it had belonged to Hannah's great granny. I was surely skeptical of it all, teasing Hannah for her superstitious beliefs. But sure enough, it performed on cue.

The wood heart-shaped planchette moved about the board spelling out answers to our questions about the supposed ghosts that haunted the public housing where Hannah and her family lived. Then when I asked my own questions, the bloody thing had worked, spelling out short answers only I could have known. At the time, I didn't understand it all. Thought it was a sort of board game, like Monopoly or Parcheesi. But that wasn't all of it.

At one point a Voice, low and growly, sounded from some-where, spouting garbled gibberish. We ran screaming from the basement room in hysterics before darting upstairs to her room and collapsing in a laughing fit in her bed.

I had never seen anything like it, and initially chalked up the experience to the pair of joints Hannah had swiped from her brother's stash. But the more we toyed with the device over the coming months, the more she wanted to plumb the depths of its secrets. But it didn't end there.

I was curious with what had occurred that evening at the sleepover. The door had cracked open, and then wider still through more experiences. I purchased some healing crystals and books on magic at a local High Street store.

That bloomin' wind picked up its pace again, sending a chill through my coat even as the memory sent a chill through my very soul. I turned the corner for the final block when I heard the *burr, burr* of a horn across the way.

"Bourne!" a voice called from a candy red BMW Z3, top down and music blaring. Sounded like *The Cure*, which could only be one person.

I laughed and raced to her car. "Hannah!"

"Hop in, girl!"

I threw open the door and sank into the creamy leather that had caused not a small amount of envy since she had gotten the car from her dad for her birthday. The heat was blowing, the music blaring, and off she went once I closed my door.

Hannah was wearing a slinky, tight-fitting dress of the Union Jack, a red cutting down her middle and across her waist against the navy blue and intersected diagonally by more red and white.

"Is that your costume?" I asked as she drove onward.

"Oh course! What did you think it was?"

"Your second job? A little red-light district, if you know what I mean. Who are you supposed to be, anyway? One of the Spice Girls?" I said laughing.

She grinned, saying nothing, those red locks of hers telling the rest of the story.

"Ginger Spice..." I said, laughing again. "You would."

"And who are you? Margaret Thatcher?" she sneered.

I frowned, saying nothing, the two of us a perfect contrast.

Then she had a roaring laugh, covering her mouth and nearly driving us off the bloomin' road.

"You are the Prime Minister, aren't you then?"

"Maybe," I mumbled, the neighborhood terrace houses drifting into High Street buildings. Changing the subject, I said, "So where is this party of yours anyhow?"

Hannah grinned. "It's a surprise."

"No..." I complained. "I hate your surprises."

"Oh, come off of it. You know you love it when I give you a good jolt out of your stogy idea of fun."

I frowned, smacking her shoulder. "When you give me a fright, more like it."

"Be careful what you wish for."

We drove on, the heat blasting our faces even as the autumn wind whooshing over the Bimmer even as The Cure continued ballading away. Soon we were far out of the country and turning off into a country road, lined with dry stone walling enclosing grassy fields that hadn't been put to agricultural use in ages. I couldn't make sense of it, and I knew better to pester Hannah about it. Best to let it play out—until she turned down a gravel road.

I sat forward, my breath catching in my chest with fright.

"Bloody hell..."

Hannah squealed. "Exactly!"

I turned to her, mouth open and wide eyes searching for answers.

She shrugged, simply saying: "We're here..."

Hannah pulled into a lot scattered with similar high-end automobile makes. It was dark, but for a clear sky with stars strewn about and a full-harvest moon shining down from above. There was also a curious orange glow coming from one end of the field.

"Where are we?" I asked, my stomach beginning to flutter with apprehension.

Hannah opened her door and stepped out. "Come on, then."

She closed her door and ran off into the night.

"Hannah!" I called out, then huffed. Just like here, the trickster she was, to drag my bum to some sodding spectacle out in the woods in the dead of night.

But I chased after her, like always.

The air was colder now, and the wind had died some. What leaves still clung to their trees rustled from a forest buttressing the property, naked limbs looking as if they were Ents clawing for me under the bright moonlight.

Climbing over a broken wooden gate doing a poor job guarding the property, I now saw the fuller measure of where my bloomin' mate had taken me.

It looked like the orange glow was coming from an abandoned farm, a large barn with a sagging roof and weather-worn gray wood anchored at one end of the lot. Hannah was running toward it, and she was shouting at me now to follow. An equally decrepit two-story white farmhouse sat several meters away. The front porch had sunk to one side in a wicked palsy, and one part of the roof was exposed to the elements, boards missing and a tree growing up its center. It smelled of decay and grass and earth, along with the curious scent of burning oil in the distance.

The place gave me the creeps, but off I went. I drew closer to the barn, the door much clearer now and the orange glow much more pronounced, when a thumping sound caught me in the chest. Not my heart, though that was beating to a bloomin' mad beat. A drum, the rhythmic *dum-ditty-dum-ditty-dum-dum-*

dum sending all the hairs across my arms standing on edge with fright.

Hannah disappeared into the glowing maw, and soon I was joining her.

Not at all prepared for what I would find, the sight seizing me like a pair of cattle prods.

The barn was cleared of hay and animals, those having long since been abandoned anyway. In their place were torches flickering with orange flames, the oil scent I had caught scent of earlier stronger now. At the center was a stone altar. Not high and table-like, but low and more like a circular platform. And there it was, anchored to the back and on the platform itself: a pentacle. A talisman used in black magic to invoke and conjure the spirits of darkness and the sigil of Baphomet adopted by Satanists.

The Horned King, the Prince of Beasts, the Lord of Demons. Satan himself.

The thrumming continued from a pair of men before large kettledrums, a low, steady beat.

Dum-ditty-dum. Dum-ditty-dum.

Others wearing black robes had arrived before us, carrying torches ablaze and held aloft. This was definitely no Halloween party.

What was Hannah thinking? And why hadn't she told her about it all?

"What is this?" I said on a shaky breath, not at all hiding my positively frightening horror at the scene splayed in front of me.

"A Black Mass service put on by a local Wiccan outfit."

"What?" I exclaimed under my breath, fearing I would disturb the forces swirling around me and call down their attention. I whipped my head toward her, continuing: "Are you serious?"

Hannah smirked, her lips almost curling back with wicked

intent. "You're not scared, are you? Or one of those religious freaks?"

I swallowed and put on my best dismissing grin. "No, of course not. But from what I know of the...service, as you put it, it's some sort of occult practice currying the favor of Satan."

She grinned. "I know! Isn't it fab?"

"You're bloomin' mad!" And I knew more than I let on.

From what I had read in my research the past few months, the service is the heart of the satanic and a direct assault against the person and work of Jesus Christ himself. It seeks to make a mockery of the bread and cup used in the Church's service of the Eucharist or Communion—the bread standing for Jesus' body, the cup of wine for his blood.

I went to protest, feeling an unease welling within my belly, when a man and a woman strode forth. My stomach sank to the dirty barn floorboards.

The man wore a goat's head mask, shirtless and muscles rippling with red paint splattered and smeared across his chest, an open black robe draping the rest of his body down to the floor; at least I hoped it was paint. A silk robe flowed from the woman, skin milky and blond hair braided and wrapped around her head into a pile.

I was speechless; so was Hannah, the ends of her mouth curled into a fanciful smile. It looked as though she was relishing the experience in her entirely out-of-place Union Jack Spice Girls costume.

The *dum-ditty-dum-ditty* of the drums rose into a thumping frenzy now, the robed figures accompanying the man and woman joining them in some ecstatic dance, setting the pagan mood for the last remaining hours of All Saints' Day.

But for what pagan, satanic purpose, I could only imagine.

It wasn't only the altar that set me on edge, or even the man and his goat-head mask.

It was the darkly hooded figures lurching back and forth in

an ecstatic dance, responding to the continued *dum-ditty-dum-ditty* that was growing in intensity with a religious fervor rivaling more charismatic sects of the Church, their torches waving around in the air like animistic spirits waiting to be unleashed on the night.

It was the censer that a woman in a flowing white robe was waving with rhythmic deliberation, its incense flooding the barn now in a miasma of spicy frankincense, a slice of the full harvest-moon light scything through the roof from above and dancing across the space.

It was the burnished bronze basin holding some curious pile of white, and a chalice bearing who knew resting on a stone table behind that hideous Goat Man.

All of it was a horrifying collection of highly ritualistic elements that was driving my soul to the very brink.

A rite I feared was poised to summon the darkness that had been awakened that fateful evening at Hannah's house, but on a scale far greater.

And darker.

Dum-ditty-dum-ditty the drums continued with rhythmic invitation, the robed figures continuing their ecstatic frenzy.

Dum-ditty-dum-ditty they bellowed, growing louder and faster and more intense, as if issuing a siren cipher call to the Devil himself and his army to rise and rend the world in two.

Then all at once it stopped.

No more *dum-ditty-dum-ditty* drumming; no more frenzied dance; no more waving of the censer. All that stood in its place was an eerie silence punctuated by whispering leaves and flapping flames on a breezy, frigid fall breath gusting now through the open barn door, accompanied by a fog that seemed to have been summoned from the depths of hell itself.

I held my breath and nearly held my heart's beat—waiting, intuiting, discerning what came next.

The man with the goat head appeared through a parting of

the incense and foggy miasma that had filled the barn, his black robe, edged with crimson swishing with every step, eyes blazing with a demonic fire through the hollowed-out orbs of the dead pagan symbol that set all of my hairs on end—sent my very soul into a panic.

Following him was another man now, dressed in faux priestly garments and wearing a wicked smile that played across his face with ill intent, bleached-white teeth gleaming in the torchlight. He caught my attention and drilled me with a gaze I found all at once creepy and horrifying. He looked vampiric, eyes possessed with thirst as the man took me in, consuming me with his gaze.

Behind him was the woman I had glimpsed earlier casting incense around the barn, playing the part of priestess for this pagan rite of darkness.

They were an unholy trinity. But for what wasn't yet clear.

The other figures, robed in black and hooded, formed a semi-circle around the altar area, casting illumination and ungodly, angular shadows from their torches around the barn.

I should have left then and there, consequences be damned. But I didn't.

Hannah took my hand and led us to join the others; I followed, unable to resist, even though every fiber of my being screamed to run away. Yet I felt powerless, a force seeming to draw me into the darkness.

Goat Man strode to the altar, flanked by the faux priest and woman. He rang a bell, signaling the beginning of a ceremony I knew deep in my bones would not end well.

"In nomine *Ha-Satanas*, domino Universi," Goat Man bellowed, his voice rising with unrighteous passion and echoing throughout the vast swath of last repose.

I immediately understood the Latin, having studied it in secondary school.

In the name of Satan, Lord of the Universe.

The man raised his head then lifted his arms. "Brethren! Let us celebrate our consciousness, fully leaning into the enlightened choice presented to all mankind by *Ha-Satan* himself, acknowledging that the flesh prevails and reason will triumph over slavish devotion to the Authority. Intimately knowing good and evil is within our grasp—becoming a god unto ourselves!"

The assembled arrayed in front of him, his congregation, raised their arms as one, even Hannah joined in.

"I proclaim to *Ha-Satan*," he continued, "and to the assembled, that I have sinned in ever-increasing measure through my thoughts, words, and deeds—by what I have thought in my mind and have done in my flesh."

'We agree,' the assembled intoned.

"Yet I am neither shameful nor repentant. *Never!* For to repent is human, to assert our consciousness is divine!"

'We agree!' they shouted, Hannah joining in with muttering agreement.

I turned to her, mouth agape and unable to speak—unable to move, really, having not recognized my mate!

But it was more than that—I really couldn't bloody move! Some Force seemed to be pressing against me, blooming from the front of the room and shackling me to the floorboards.

"May *Ha-Satan* guide us into full humanity," Goat Man boomed, his eyes closed and arms outstretched. "May he bless us as we partake of the bountiful pleasures bestowed by the Universe in all of their wondrous glory and open to our imbibing in full conscious awareness!"

As one, the congregants chanted: *'Ha-Satanas nobiscum!'*
Satan is with us, indeed.

"Hannah..." I squeaked, the only thing I could think to say in the face of such evil, my body immobile by that Force that pressed against me with such weight, such ferocity.

She ignored me, eyes wide and transfixed, paralytic even.

"Glory to the Lord of the Universe," Goat Man went on, "the

Angel of Light, the powerful *Ha-Satan*, the One who brings enlightenment, life and freedom, the fullness of consciousness to humankind. We bow in reverence, we give thee worth, and we give thee glory, for thou art the fullness of true Light and true Darkness, the Master of Consciousness who guides us upon the true path of enlightenment, while the religious fools of our enemy flail blindly and babble in their ignorance, following the man from Nazareth who died with pity."

'*Veni, exaltatum Ha-Satanas!*' the group shouted as one.

O come, exalted Satan!

Then Goat Man lowered his arms. "Let us pray to the one who has delivered us out of ignorance and into the marvelous light of consciousness, inviting the Angel of Light to open the eyes of our full humanity."

The white of the man's eyes disappeared, seemingly closing for some unholy prayer. His chest rose with a deep breath, then he cleared his throat and began reciting some sort of prayer I had never heard of, the others joining in with echoing memory, even Hannah:

> *Our Father who art from the depths of*
> *enlightenment, glorious be Thy Name,*
> *Thy Republic of Heaven be here, thy truth to bear*
> *On Earth, far-removed from the Kingdom of Heaven.*
> *Return to us our consciousness, and tempt us with*
> *the fullness of pleasurable humanity.*
> *For ours is the Republic of Heaven, the power, and*
> *the glory, forever and ever!*
> *Ave* Ha-Satanas!

Hail, Satan.

I had to get out of there, no matter what Hannah thought. I had to escape, find help, perhaps bring them back to rescue my friend who was entranced now.

I went to step back when a rumbling began to course through the barn. Something deep within the belly of the floor-boards itself began to well up within, grasping for the surface.

But not just within the barn.

Within Goat Man as well.

He began to tremble in mighty waves, vibrating with intensity from head to toe. He bent low and brought his arms inside, every limb twisting in at wicked angles. His fingers curled in on his palms with rigidity. His skin was beet red, as if burning a high-grade fever before bubbling into white welts of second-degree burns.

A sudden scream pierced through the barn, shooting up from his belly and out into the night. He threw back his head and arched his back, his face contorting and jaw rending itself this way and that.

And then it came.

A voice.

The Voice.

Strong and lowly, sure and proud.

The same unholy sound I had heard that fateful night at Hannah's house!

"*Behold!*" the Voice growled with intensity. "*I hath manifested amongst my children to bear witness to thy ignorance. I have come to revel in thy outrages against the Authority, and to hear your pleas for enlightened consciousness this night. Let them be declared in my name and laid at my feet.*"

The demonic incarnation scoped us all arrayed before him, men and women who were erect and all at once trembling in his presence. Something within seized my very soul as his gaze fell upon me. Something burning and terrifying, as if I would spontaneously combust from the inside right in that very barn, in that very moment.

Goat Man licked his lips and flicked his tongue at us with

desire. He raised his hands and shouted, *"May the heavens tremble at thy imprecations!"*

This was not bloomin' happening...

I strained against the Force still pressing in against me. I struggled for breath even, but it was no use. I was stuck, along with Hannah and the rest, bound and erect before the incarnation of the Devil himself.

My chest felt as if it would explode; my heart was thumping with intensity. My head was filled with an equally thumping, throbbing pressure, and a heaviness fell over me—as if the weight of the Universe had descended upon my body, holding me and suffocating me with menacing intent.

I closed her eyes and took in a deep breath, then prayed the prayer Jesus Christ himself had taught his people to pray with silent, frenzied petition. A prayer from my childhood that seemed right in the moment:

'Our Father in heaven, hallowed be your name. Your kingdom come. Your will be done, on Earth as it is in Heaven. Give us this day our daily bread. And forgive us our sins, as we also forgive those who have sinned against us. And lead us not into temptation and trial, but rescue us from—'

"Witless are those who deign to submit to the Authority," the Voice thundered through Goat Man with unholy interruption.

'—the Evil One...'

"Blinded are those who know not the gift given by Ha-Satan. *Two thousand years ago, I offered this gift to the man who would be King of kings and Lord of lords."*

A cold dread flooded my veins, jolting my heart with a caustic pop and weakening my bowels with watery worry.

The Voice continued its low and guttural intonations, masked by an otherworldly garble that smacked of supernatural manifestation.

I was undone. I was done for.

But I couldn't give in. Not for me, and not for Hannah, who was still transfixed.

A tremble ran the length of the barn beneath, as if the very ground were about to erupt with emotion. The arrayed congregation erupted in laughter, a frenzied giggling that ricocheted across the barn and grew a head of otherworldly steam until the boards themselves seemed to be dripping with condescension.

"Perhaps we should prepare the sacrifice, my liege," another voice sounded. It was the faux priest.

"Yes, prepare the host!!!" the Voice erupted.

Goat Man seemed to turn toward me, a Cheshire-cat grin splayed across that pale face of his. I thought the man would come for me, but a bleating cut through the frenzy, shaking me to the core.

The woman in white was leading a goat toward the altar.

And now I understood it.

The sacrificial lamb...

Faux Priest took the goat from the woman and hoisted it up on the altar, the poor beast giving another cry.

"As our Angel of Light revolted from up on high in righteous dissent," the man said, "we too cast aside the shackles of subjugation and the binds of the Authority with this blood of the one who rejected the Light in favor of the Authority. We will drink and find sustenance this night in the blood of a different sacrifice, writing the name of *Ha-Satan* upon our hearts in *this* blood, giving us the strength to repel the Authority and his minions, rending our foes asunder under our enlightened consciousness."

He lifted the chalice up toward the heavens, a tingling power now coursing through the room. I wondered if what had invaded Goat Man was now seeking another.

"O Children of *Ha-Satan*," he thundered, "by the blood of this reject, I incite thee to rise from tears and come to joy! From suffering, come to pleasure! From injustice, seek restitution! From injury, seek vengeance! Deny and spurn the dominion of the Authority! For thou art thy own, bought and paid by no one!"

The others intoned, *'By our own hand shall we be delivered!'*

The woman in white tolled a bell, six times in all. The mark of mankind, of the Beast that was about to be fully unleashed.

The *dum-ditty-dum-ditty* drum beat launched a heart-pounding score again that sent my head spinning with delirium—spiritual and existential—with one question on my mind.

How the bloody hell was I going to get out of this one?

The man withdrew from his robes a knife, the blade shimmering in the firelight with a handle of ivory encrusted with jewels.

A ceremonial athame blade, used to slay a sacrifice for the gods.

The drum beat was beating in a *dum-ditty-dum-ditty* frenzy now, the onlookers dressed in black robes swaying and their arms wrenching this way and that in a state of ecstatic possession.

"Children of enlightenment, unchained from Christian duty," Goat Man said, voice guttural and growly, *"the blessing of Ha-Satan be upon thee. In the full authority and enlightenment of the Angel of Light, I release you to topple tradition and dance upon its rubble! For verily, give glory to no one but your own consciousness—in body, mind, and soul. For you have been freed from the Authority. And whom the Beast has set free, is free indeed!"*

A tremble took hold of me now, the spiritual weight of the Voice pressing in against me in a way I had never before felt. And Goat Man was now staring straight at me.

I felt suddenly exposed, insignificant even, as the eyes bore into me, and I knew I was looking straight into the presence of pure evil.

Then bowing his head, Goat Man suddenly held the athame blade aloft above the goat now bound upon the altar, its surface glinting with unholy, murderous intent in the firelight.

The Voice returned, first with a barkish, sneering laugh. Then he said, *"With this blood, the mighty, full of consciousness and choice, shall inherit the earth, liberated through the power of blood and sacrifice!"*

Stepping back, Goat Man continued holding the knife above the altar, ready for the dreadful moment of sacrifice. The drumbeat grew louder, more furious, the *dum-ditty-dum-ditty* rising with a thumping fury.

I hated any sort of violence, especially against animals. I couldn't bear to watch. And yet I felt I could do nothing otherwise.

"Jesus, no…"

Suddenly, something inside me broke. The power, the Force that had been pressing in against me and holding me steady seemed to loosen its hold.

The man pulled the knife higher, as if ready to thrust it down upon the goat.

"Oh, Jesus…"

Again, the Force lessened, the pull loosened.

Then it hit me.

The name. That's what did it.

The name of Jesus!

So I said it again, more confident this time.

"Jesus, help."

Now it was really unraveling, as if cords of rope that had bound me tight had completely gone limp, unfurling from my hands and feet, lying in a pile beneath me.

I backed away, able to take a step now. The leaden-weight sensation was nearly gone.

The *dum-ditty-dum-ditty* of the drum was ratcheted to a

frenzied state now. The moment was nigh, the goat offering a mournful bleat as if anticipating it.

So I grabbed Hannah's arms and tugged for her to go.

She wouldn't budge.

I tugged some more, wrapping my fingers around her arm and yanking with purpose.

She gave, stumbling into me.

"What the bloody hell—"

She sounded drunk, high even. Intoxicated on the power manifesting that night.

Which meant I had little choice in the matter for what came next.

Without explaining, I wrapped my arm in hers and pulled her with all my might, dragging her toward the door.

She kicked and screamed some, but she had little power of her own, her own volition having been sapped amongst the crowd of onlookers.

We reached the entrance, and I lunged for the outside still lit white by the moon, leaving behind the darkness for the light. When we did, a sudden sick bleat of death screamed out from behind, one final desperate plea for help.

I knew what had happened, which spurred me onward back toward Hannah's car. She continued protesting with weak fits as I dragged her along, but I managed. Soon I was hoisting her over the decrepit wooden gate and tossing her inside the passenger's seat.

By now, she had passed out completely. From what, I could not say. Again, perhaps a hangover from the intoxication of pure evil, but I wasn't certain. All I knew was that I was desperate to leave, desperate to get back home to Mum and sob away all that had transpired.

With shaking hands, I fished for Hannah's keys. Success. Soon, we were motoring onto the main road with the squeal of tires racing back home to safety.

Leaving the darkness behind for good.

Speeding away from that place, hair whirling and tears burning cold against my cheeks in the wind, the only thing I could think to do was pray the name who had seemed to loosen the bindings of the Devil himself.

Jesus. Jesus.

Then again: *Jesus. Jesus.*

Still more: *Jesus. Jesus!*

I hoped he heard my pleas for help. Something deep down assured me he had—and answered them that night.

The return trip was a silent one, neither of us speaking. Neither of us much wanting to; me more than Hannah, who still seemed hung over by the encounter. Finally reaching her home, I parked the Bimmer and helped Hannah to the front door. She stumbled inside, neither of us saying a word about what had happened.

Walking the several blocks I still had to traverse home, alone and stumbling, a story I'd heard from a few years ago popped into my head along the way. One about Jesus driving a demon from a possessed man. The story had fascinated me in part because of the window it gave into a fantastical dimension outside of our normal world—of spirits and angels influencing our affairs, our lives even.

As the Gospel of Luke recounts, chapter 4, Jesus rebuked the demon saying, *'Be silent, and come out of him!'* The demon threw the man down and came out of him, and all who looked on were amazed, wondering about Jesus: *'What kind of utterance is this? For with authority and power he commands the unclean spirits, and out they come!'*

"Be silent, and come out of me!" was what I wanted to scream, feeling as if something had been sparked within, a rift opening up inside my very soul into the dark realm of which this story from the Gospels spoke.

That night I had seen the reality of Satan made flesh. The

Devil was real; so was his power. But I had learned something more.

I learned the power of Jesus' name in a way I hadn't before. That power, that *Name*, had been far greater than the Voice made manifest in that dreadful barn.

I will never forget it.

And I hope I will never encounter that dreadful Voice again, as long as I shall live.

4. LIFE ROLLS BY GOD'S GRACE
(MATT GAPINKSI)

I stumbled into the room and got to work. Not my idea of a fabulous, funtastic Friday night. But when duty calls, you sign on the dotted lines and say 'Where to?'

So there I was, throwing open the door in pitch blackness at the call of duty. Literally, the yelping pluckin' my ever livin' nerves as I swooped in for the save. Which really shouldn't have been all that heroic, given what I'd signed up for. And definitely shouldn't have been pluckin' my ever livin' nerves, given who it was I was coming in to help.

But at two in the morning, with how much my aching backside really needed a good night sleep—the little dude's antics were not appreciated, especially on my day off from SEPIO drama. But I'd volunteered to man the post should the little dude throw up a squall of protest.

And protest and squall he did!

So I tried what I usually did, getting down on all fours and singing silly songs. Then I did a little dance and tried talking him through it all.

Again, no go.

Still squalling, and now squirming to beat the band!

Then I had it:

Food!

I chuckled to myself as I left the little guy still squalling and squirming while I rustled up some goods. Of course, why didn't I think of that sooner? Me, king of the eats! Us Gapinskis were bred that way, after all. Big-boned bruisers.

I returned and offered the little dude what I'd prepared, since other accommodations weren't immediately available, and he took to it.

"There we go…"

Then I settled in for night duty while he ate, yawning as my mind drifted to this, that, and the other thing.

Like God's providential sovereignty.

Not sure why, in that moment while the little dude ate and I kept watch. But also, why not? Certainly had time to kill. What better thing to think about in the wee hours of the morning than trying to solve the theological conundrum that's vexed Christians stretching back two millennia?

I stood as the little dude kept at it, mulling it over in my noggin' at the butt-crack of dawn. Not even dawn; that was still three hours away!

"It's like most things in life, right?" I said to no one in particular—especially the little dude I was keeping watch over; way over his head! But his little peepers glanced my way as he chugged, so I went with it. "A funny combination of luck and God's providential intervention. Though I tend to err on the side of the Almighty poking his finger in our business more than just fate messing with us."

I snorted a chuckle. "Believe me, I, Matthew Gapinski, would know more than most."

No reaction from the little dude, which I guess was a good thing. Didn't want to scare him off so soon.

"Then again, so would most of the dudes and dudettes in the Bible, now that i think of it. Or maybe all of them."

I bobbed up and down and changed arms, the guy seeming to lose interest as he kept chugging.

"Take Joseph," I said. "Not Jesus' pops—or rather, his adoptive dad, or whatever, since God is, like, the dad of Jesus. God the Father, God the Son, and all. But you wouldn't understand that yet."

The little dude gave a burp, which was progress.

"Anyway, I meant Joseph and the technicolor dream coat variety. The one who got the raw end of the family stick. Youngest of eleven sons of Jacob, and grandson of Isaac, and great-grandsons of Abraham—the dude who started this whole Abrahamic faiths business. Judaism, Christianity, Islam. Which would turn my Southern Baptist Grandpappy over in his grave if he heard me bunching them all up in the same family tree, with Christianity and all."

I chuckled, but the little dude wasn't in on the joke. One day, maybe...

"Anyway, that guy. The one favored by his pops Jacob. To the point of getting that sweet technicolor dream coat as a gift one day, setting all his bros on edge and priming the pump for what came later. There's your Exhibit A."

I returned to the task at hand, the little guy seemingly enjoying himself now.

"As the venerable Stephen King likes to say: Great events turn on small hinges. Or in my case, the worm turns when God sneezes. At least, that's what it seems like half the time."

Then I cocked my head, bobbing on my knees now to try and get the little dude to speed this thing along.

"Although now I think it's closer to the idea that life rolls by on God's grace. Sometimes life rolls over you. But most of the time you're being carried along as life rolls on by—and all of it is by the grace of God. His crazy love for us."

Not half bad, Gapinski...

Switching arms, I continued, "Anyway, back to Joe, who

goes on to have these wicked dreams about eleven sheaves of grain bowing down to himself, and then the moon and sun and eleven stars bowing down to him as well. His brothers and pops Jacob got the hint. They'd kiss his feet one day."

Another arm switch. "Which pretty well set everything else in motion for what came next. Because one day, our man Joe was sent to offer a little hidey-ho to his bros on behalf of pops —every older bros annoyance. Leading to Exhibit B. And really, Exhibits B through D!"

Because, again, as my man King says: Great events turn on small hinges.

I sat down now, dog tired from the midnight snack. "So there's Joe, traipsing from their hometown through the countryside, sent by pops to get his brothers for lunch. Yet they're not where they're supposed to be. But there just so happens to be some dude who knows where they are."

Exhibit B.

"Then when Joe fetches said bros, they turn on him, catching sight of him in the distance and plotting to get rid of this technicolor-dream-coat-wearing bro of theirs. But the oldest objects and thinks they should throw him instead in...oh, a large pit that just so happens to be chilling a klick away."

Exhibit C.

"Theeenn, just as the bros are deliberating over what to do about young Joe, a caravan of a bunch of dudes straight out of Arabian Nights just happens to come trotting on by."

Annnd Exhibit D.

"Which is just crazy!" I chuckled, startling the little dude. I sucked in a worried breath, praying to the good Lord above that he didn't start wailing! But he recovered and went back to his midnight snack—a true Gapinski!

"Anyway, then off he goes into the wild blue yonder before another series of unfortunate events unfold—Exhibits F through Z—before the dude is made Pharaoh's right-hand man."

I started rocking in the chair now, thinking more about the story. "But at this junction, before all the other crazy unfolds, there's this nugget: *'The Lord was with Joseph, and he became a successful man...'*"

I stopped rocking and sat up with a thought.

Maybe Sir King should be amended slightly: Great events turn on the Lord's providential intervention.

Or better: Great events hinge on God's *withness*.

"Hey, that's pretty good! Sounds about right." I chuckled again, the little dude stirring, about to pitch a fit now. "No, no, no. Sorry to disturb the force, my little dude. Get back to it..."

And he did. Without a fuss, thank the Lord Almighty!

I sighed and stood, thinking back over my brilliance, and returning to what I had thought before. That it was more like it that life rolls by the grace of God.

"I'd know more than most," I mumbled. "With firsthand experience. The fact I'm alive is Exhibit A!"

Now the little dude looked at me, fixing me with eyes curious for more.

I took a breath and sighed, not wanting to get into it. At least not yet.

But there they were—those little orbs of infinite curiosity and love fixed on me with interest.

Which gave me just enough courage to spill the beans.

"Let me back it up a bit. Because you might as well know now, while the gettin's good." Switching arms again, I continued, "I came from what you might call a broken home. Well, not broken, per se. More like a royally effed-up house, pardon the French. Momma and Pops were still together, but they went at it like cats and dogs, like roosters and hens—mixing about as well as antifreeze and transmission fluid, which will royally jack up your car, by the way. Believe, I know. And I've got the broken arm to prove it after I tried helping pops out."

I took a breath and nodded. Pretty well about summed up my childhood.

"Pops was a drunk who was a four-time loser after his fourth and final stab at shooting for the middle class was roundly defeated after his bossman caught him stealing a sip of Jackie D out of a beaten up aluminum flask leftover from Nam, right after stealing a few Jeffersons out from the petty cash. Claimed it had all been a misunderstanding, but the Universe knew better. Yet Pops insisted life kept beating him down. So he beat me down when there wasn't anyone else around but himself to blame."

Little guy let out a nice Gapinski-style belch. I braced for what came next, but was safe. No projectiles this round!

Sighing with relief, I continued, "Now Momma wasn't much better. Hooked on opioids before that was a thing and confined me to my basement room when I dropped a Cheerio on her nice clean double-wide floor. And yes, in case you were wondering if our mobile home did have a basement, us Gapinski's lived in trailer-trash style!"

I settled into the chair again, getting dog tired now from the trip down memory lane and wishing little dude would finish up.

"You can imagine," I went on, "that life pretty well sucked to high heaven with the kinds of parents I had. Which pretty much made every other part of life suck. One thing led to another...Well, several things led to another, and before I knew it, I was a high school dropout who wanted nothing to do with the world. Nothing to do with life."

I took a breath, uncertain about continuing. Then I glanced down at the little dude, those eyes still staring at me, as if wanting me to go on. So I did.

"About the only thing that kept me alive—literally, as it will become clear soon—was my Grandpappy Gapinski. Now, Grandpappy was more like a dad than Pops ever was. And actually, he played the part of Momma pretty dang well, too. Picked me up from school when both were too drunk or too stoned to do so. Taught me how to drive and how to change a tire, how to shave and calculate the airspeed velocity of an unladen sparrow—in that order."

I chuckled at the memory, my throat growing thick with emotion and my peepers threatening to overflow with all grandpappy had done for me—what he meant to me! Just wished he was still around to teach me how to parent...

Staring off into the ceiling, I noticed the little dude didn't startle now. Which meant he must be quite content—and close to dreamland. Perfect!

"In fact," I went on, "you could call him Exhibit B of the goodness of God I was talking about. How life is a funny combination of luck and God's providential intervention. Because if it weren't for God gifting me that man, I'd be a goner. Literally, because, one afternoon while Momma and Pops were both passed out, I strung myself up from the neck and kicked a bucket out from underneath me."

I frowned, looking back into those few-month old eyes. "I know. Cuckoo for Cocoa Puffs. And a complete dumb—" I stopped short, nearly letting my potty mouth slip in front of the little dude. So I went with: "Baby's bottom. Anyway, only problem was, I did it wrong. Too much slack in the rope. And when the bucket went one way, I went down but not out. Which was pretty much par for the course for most things I set my mind to. Might as well as biffed it trying to exit this world, right?"

Little dude was stirring again, so I stood back up and started bobbing on the knees. "Yet, I like to see it as the Lord Almighty reaching down into my story and messing up my carefully laid plans. Maybe stretching the rope out a bit or zapping the bucket a size bigger before I was done prepping."

More stirring, so I switched arms again. "Either way, the way it worked out was not like I'd planned it...thank the Lord for that! So there I went. Only thing was, the rope still tightened around my neck just so. And instead of snapping it in two, I was left standing on my tiptoes! Then the other thing about it was, I couldn't do jack with the rope above. Just pirouetting on my tiptoes on the cold concrete, face turning purple while my chubby fingers were straining against the rope taut like chicken wire around my neck leading to the pipe above."

I stopped, wondering if I should continue given what came next.

Looking back down, those eyes told me all I needed to know: Continue.

So I did. Back to bobbing and weaving across the floor. Mostly out of nerves for sharing a part of me that only four other people in the entire world knew about.

Back to it: "So there I was, twistin' and turnin' on the rope and my toes, gripping it with both hands above and trying to escape all Houdini style while pretty much choking to death. But not so much that I was actually dying. Air was hard to come by, but somehow I clung to consciousness, which was sure to fade quickly. Then I heard the door open above. Kitchen door that led to the covered carport, smacking against the counter like it always did. Then a few hollers from a familiar voice before the floorboards above started barking."

I stopped, staring out into the darkened room humming with the silence of the night, the memories haunting me now in a way they hadn't in years.

Swallowing hard, I took a breath. He deserved to know. So I continued: "You see, Grandpappy had showed up carrying an extra large Pizza Hut Meat Lover pizza. Smelled him before I heard him, all those pepperonis and Italian sausages, chunks of ham and bacon, seasoned pork and beef wafting down below on a hot August breeze. Can still remember the floorboards creaking above and his Southern hollers echoing through the double-wide while I continued my dance, the remaining spark of life inside wanting nothing more than to get out of that noose and pretend like things were alright—if nothing more from sheer embarrassment than some remaining ember that still wanted to live. Still wanted to breathe in that stale, moldy basement air and eat that pizza piled high with meat that would give a moose a coronary."

That King quote came back: Great events turn on small hinges.

I shook my head. Life rolls by God's grace, that's what.

"It was purely by the grace of God that Grandpappy walked through the door and found me the way I was. Must have seen my twinkle toes dancing in the open door, because next thing I knew, I was being saved."

Bobbing again, I explained to the little dude in a whisper now, "Purely by the grace of God that you, the little dude in my arms, are around to hear me tell my sad tale about my sad life."

Scratch that.

Sad *former* life.

Because I explained, retelling the tale: "The pizza went first, dropping like a sack of potatoes before tumbling down the stairs, the box opening wide like a frightened mouth before the whole dang pizza tumbled down in a big, fat waste. Then Grandpappy hustled on the double, nearly leaping down the full length of the stairwell before grabbing me by the chest and heaving me high while he somehow managing to untie the mess of knots I'd made above my head."

My throat suddenly grew thick with emotion. I swallowed, knowing the truth of the crazy ordeal: Grandpappy saved my life.

In more ways than one...

Putting the little dude on my shoulder now, I continued, "That day, literally after he revived me and then smacked me upside the head for even contemplating exiting this life after nearly squeezing the life out of me while bawling a bucket of tears no man, or woman for that matter, had ever cried over me —that day he carried me out of that house with a cotton pickin' rope burn ringing my neck, he filed for custody with the court, and got me the hell out of Dodge. Raised me up to be the man that I am."

First of many Joe moments, little dude. The first of many great events that turned on small hinges. Those events that hinged on God's *withness*.

"Now, I suppose one could make the argument, little dude, that the Lord Almighty messed up in the first place by birthing me from the loins of two parents who were never in their lives going to earn Parent of the Year awards. Could argue God sneezed when the pair were getting it on after dinner out on their second wedding anniversary."

Maybe.

"But I like to think God was with me from well before that, when Pops's pops became a Southern Baptist minister, training and preparing for the day he would step in to save me from the hell my dad unleashed on me."

A small cry erupted from my arms, which was fine because they were getting dog tired after feeding and then bobbing little Matt Junior up and down for the past hour.

Maybe this would help…

I switched the kid to my other shoulder. Poor thing had had a rough time falling to sleep after mama fed him for the midnight feeding; must not have been fully full. Again: big-boned bruisers, that's us Gapinskis!

Bobbing up and down on my knees again, rubbing the little guy's back and patting it, I smiled, thinking about the tiny bundle of joy starting to snore on my shoulder now.

"And you know what, Matt Junior? You'd be Exhibit Q. Yes, you are, my little peanut."

Great events turn on small hinges, King says. But I knew it was more than that: Life rolls by on God's grace.

The times that life comes rolling up to you with job offers and true love and little peanuts snoring in breathy starts and grandpappy's randomly paying a visit when you're dangling from the end of a suicide gone bad.

As well as the times that life comes steamrolling over you with cancer diagnoses and unemployment and eviction and crappy drunk, drugged-out parents who don't give a damn about no one but themselves—the good and bad life rolls, great and small life events, all of 'em turn on small hinges riding on the grace of God.

It's all grace, all the way down.

I'm proof of that.

And you are Matt Junior. As well as your mama snoozing in the next room.

5. STRANGELY WARMED (SILAS GREY)

I jumped out of the Humvee and stormed after the guy who was in my crosshairs since they'd hauled butt after a pair of Black Hawks came in hot and heavy to cover their escape—moving from a walk to a skip to a run toward the cowboy who thought he was all that. Apparently, the knuckle-head thought his way of doing things out in the field under heavy fire was better than his commanding officer.

Which happened to be me, Silas Grey. *Sergeant* Grey to the private from somewhere south of the Mason-Dixon who'd gotten mouthy. Them types were always from south of the Mason-Dixon. Although the hotshots from up both coasts could give just as much lip. It was the boys from the middle of America, fly-over country the suits on TV called it, that usually were the best behaved. Especially when the bullets started whizzing by and every second, every *order*, counted.

The guy named Bobby John Walker—if that ain't a good ol' boy name from the Deep South, I don't know what is—stepped out of a dark-green M35 cargo truck we'd been using to haul a cache of seized weapons from a small town an hour outside our camp, Camp Liberty, just outside Baghdad. I was beelining it for the guy with all the pent-up firepower inside those mounted M2 machine guns and Mk 19 grenade launchers on the M35.

Mostly because I was ticked at him not following orders to disengage, the showboat trying to score some points but picking off a few easy shots that flared up the hornet's nest that forced us to call in air support in the first place—and risking the lives of the rest of my crew.

The other side of it was that '*Yee-haw*' shout of victory he'd let loose when he dismounted the truck, as if what he'd pulled had just won Operation Iraqi Freedom all by himself, as if he'd toppled those Saddam statues or yanked the Grand Poobah from that hole in the ground.

And I was hot as all get out, sweating to beat the band, mouth tasting of salt from the perspiration running down my face and gritty from the sand still trapped in my mouth from that windstorm stirred up from the Black Hawks that had to save our asses. I was neither a happy camper nor comfortable camper.

So I wanted a pound of fresh. And blood.

"What the hell were you thinking!" I yelled as I walked up to the kid only a few years younger than me.

Bobby John spun around, that cocky grin still splayed across that square-jawed baby face wrapped around that underdeveloped brain that got me in that mood in the first place.

He shrugged. "What?"

What? *Really?* That's all the kid could say after defying a direct order?

Should have just ran his ass then and there through the Uniformed Code of Military Justice for the insubordination in the field. Let them deal with it.

But, again, I was hot and sweaty and my mouth was still filled with that blasted sand thanks to his showboating!

So I cocked him one straight into his kisser, the ridgeline of his nose cracking and blood instantly blooming and a few teeth probably loosening. The poor fella from south of the Mason-Dixon stumbled back and landed flat on his backside, a plume of dust from the parched ground rising with an exclamation point.

Little did I realize, but Major Pepper was walking up behind me, on his way to another engagement but seeing all he needed to see to run my own ass through the Uniformed Code of Military Justice for attacking a fellow soldier.

He quickly pulled me out as Bobby John staggered to his feet to fend for his manhood, easing the private down and taking me aside before it went any further. Which I half appreciated but half resented, wanting to go toe to toe with the guy after what he had pulled.

"What the hell was that about, GREY?!" the Major asked, bald head sending up a flair of reflective sun cresting right and good toward the horizon.

I went to bite back, but bit my tongue instead. Literally, closing my mouth in the process to shut me up and shut me down before I made matters worse.

But then he forced my hand: *"ANSWER ME SOLDIER!!"*

So I did. "The guy's an immature jackass who doesn't follow orders and doesn't deserve to wear the Ranger's name—*sir!*"

"And who doesn't deserve to be part of your platoon?"

I went to yell *"Heck yeah, sir!"* when I realized the man had goaded me.

The Major took a breath then rested a hand on my shoulder, looking me square in the face. Sort of creeped me out, the man coming in close in a way I hadn't seen him before. But he didn't give me much time to think about it.

"Look, Grey, I'll deal with him later. Walker is a good soldier with high marks, but is a bit too big for his britches at times." Then he leaned in even closer, saying lowly: "I also know the man joined your team as a replacement to Green. I know you two were close, and it was a right shame what happened to the guy. I also know you've been struggling to come to grips with—"

"Sir, I'm fine," I interrupted.

He pulled back and put up a hand. "Save it, Sergeant. I know you are, but I also know you're not. Frankly, neither would I be after the hell you went through."

A group of men passed us, heads down and the setting sun casting long shadows across their faces and burnt brown sand.

"You and I both know you haven't been yourself. You've been out of focus and missing details, been more ornery of late and mouthing back even to me."

I felt heat rising from the back of my neck with embarrassment as much as anger at the accusations. Probably true, but didn't care for them in the slightest.

"Not bustin' your balls here, Grey, just stating the obvious. And now with the blowup between you and Walker—"

"But sir—" I protested, stiffening and feeling like I needed to launch into a full-throated defense of myself, and feeling like the man thought of me less-than for what had happened on that road to Mosul those weeks ago.

"*SAVE IT GREY!*" he shouted, cutting me off as another batch of privates shuffled past, heads down at the outburst. "And take the night. I know you're on duty, posted at the gate, but you need to get your head on straight. And that's an order!"

I widened my stance and held my head. It had been that obvious. I was that broken. Then I clenched my jaw and steadied my breath to stay my rising heart rate, feeling like the biggest failure ever—not being able to keep my stuff together after it all went down with Colton. What would Dad have thought?

Major Pepper took a breath and sighed, brushing a hand across his skinhead. "I lost a good man myself, back in the first Gulf War."

I raised my head, coming eye to eye with the man who'd never uttered a single self-revealing word in the year I'd been under his command.

He continued, "Messed me up something fierce, Grey. Didn't have a name for it back then. PTSD, they call it now. And I'd advise you to keep a close watch on whatever it is that's going on inside of you—whatever it is that's busting out into the open. For our sake, for yours. Because it will eat you alive."

Then a shudder ran through the man, and he clenched his jaw and stiffened. "You've got twelve hours to shape up, soldier! Use the time wisely. Don't make me ship you out."

And with that, Major Pepper strolled off to harass a group of men slouching against a Humvee, one man's shirt untucked and ordering them to drop and give him fifty.

I watched him leave, mumbling a "Yessir," before slumping away into the waning daylight cresting into evening.

Couldn't believe I'd been sidelined like that. Although, I would probably can my ass too after what I'd pulled with Walker. Was for my own good, and the Major knew that. Knew he was looking out for me. Kinda weird as I thought more about it, especially him opening up like that. Felt less alone and more...normal? Made sense, given what I'd been through. But it was more than that.

A rowdy bunch of boys hooted and hollered in a group up the way, cheering about something I couldn't care less about. But one thing was for sure: I felt the least normal and the most alone I'd felt in years.

Had always been the life of the party, actually, surrounded by lots of people and teammates from sports, although I wasn't sure I'd call any of them friends. In fact, didn't have much growing up. Was more surrounded by people than I was involved with people. Same on base, now that I thought about it. Probably the fault of having risen quickly to sergeant, standing out among the others and over them in command. Leadership was lonely at the top, they say. Ain't that right!

But it was the normal side of things that probably had something to do with it, never feeling like I belonged, always on the outside even though I'd been the life of the party and part of the 'in' crowds through high school at Falls Church High and into college at Georgetown University. Funny how that happens. How you can be surrounded by people, be part of all the right circles, and still feel the most alone and the least normal.

I took in a breath of the night air and continued heading nowhere in particular, the humid heat lifting some and the scents of roasted meat and mint and baked bread coming in on a cool breeze from somewhere that made my mouth water for a good, home-cooked meal. Made me long for home, too, a memory of Dad grilling lamb chops and garnishing them with some crushed mint and mango thing he'd concocted, with a side of roasted bulgur wheat that Sebastian and I thought was interesting enough, if not a bit overdone and too garlicky. Thankfully, hopping around bases with Dad over the years as children had refined our pallets more than most teenagers. So goat with a mint-mango hash and bulgur wheat didn't turn our stomachs.

But I also knew better.

Because while my brother and I got to see the world, we'd never had roots. Never had people to call our own and pal around with. Never had community, other than the fellow Army brats, but they hardly liked us since we were always the new kids on the block, having jumped around so often. And Dad was a Major General, so that always went over well.

Maybe it made sense, then, that I felt so alone even now, so abnormal and removed from it all. So alien from the world—from myself, even.

Something caught my attention. Music.

No, it wasn't so much tunes floating along the evening air. It was more than that.

It was singing, an odd sound on an Iraqi base!

"What the..." I muttered, following the off-key trail of notes floating along the renewed breeze of that roasted meat and mint and baked bread.

It was coming from a tent at one end of the dirt road slicing through camp.

Ahh. The local chapel, staffed by the super-religious chaplains supplied by the military. Some Catholic, from my home team, some Jewish, some Protestant, of what they call the "evangelical" variety.

I scoffed and kept walking, literally turning my nose up at the canvas hall erected to host religious gatherings, even Mass, which I never attended. Hadn't been to one regularly since childhood, and even in college only went sporadically.

But then I heard it. A song, connected to a memory. Couldn't place it entirely, but the opening line grabbed me by the ears and wouldn't let me keep walking:

'Amazing grace, How sweet the sound...'

Someone was belting it above the rest, or amplified enough by Army-issued sound equipment to carry my way.

'That saved a wretch like me' the song continued on as I stood still on the packed sand in the waning evening.

The guy leading the charge could hold a tune, at least. The others who were following along...not so much.

'I once was lost, but now I am found, was blind, but now I see.'

Emotion suddenly sprang to the corners of my eyes. Which was super weird, since I hadn't cried much since childhood either. Not even at pop's funeral after those damn planes—

Pop's funeral...

That's why I'd recognized it. We sang it at his graveside service. Was his favorite song. More memories rushed to the surface of Dad humming it at the spartan desk in our on-base housing, paying bills or taking care of Army business, whistling the tune underneath the car changing the oil, even singing it in the shower, which was an experience.

I chuckled at the memory, a song I'd heard growing up suppressed and now finding its way into some chapel service on some base in the middle of some desert in Iraq. Unbelievable.

Another stanza yanked me from my trip down memory lane, starting back up:

> *Through many dangers, toils and snares*
> *I have already come,*
> *'Tis grace has brought me safe thus far*
> *And grace will lead me home.*

Now they had me, that refrain repeating itself and reaching in deep—soul deep: *'Through many dangers, toils and snares I have already come.'*

Are you kidding me? Seemed a bit too on point. But the idea that God's grace had brought me safe thus far...and a grace that would lead me home? Tell that to Dad, tell that to all the others who'd died and gone to who-knew-where.

"Tell that to Colton..." I muttered, throat constricting with emotion now.

The name felt sour in my mouth. I swallowed hard then gathered some saliva, sending it sailing to the ground in an arc of spittle at the idea.

I smirked and shook my head, then said goodbye with a wave-off, turning back toward...wherever it was I was walking, which I didn't recall. Straight to nowhere, because that's where I felt I was headed.

But something wouldn't let me. Maybe it was the song, or the memory attached to it; maybe it was Dad himself, the saint he was reaching down through Saint Pete's pearly gates to grab me by the neck and drag me inside. Wouldn't put it past him!

For some reason, I crossed myself—hadn't done that in years, either. Whether for confirmation or protection, didn't know. All I knew, deep down, was that I needed to be in that chapel service. Didn't know in the slightest. Just a feeling I couldn't shake.

So I sauntered to the entrance, peeling back a flap of canvas serving as a door and leaning against a support post just as the final stanza started:

> *When we've been there ten thousand years*
> *Bright shining as the sun,*
> *We've no less days to sing God's praise*
> *Than when we've first begun.*

Another bout of emotion sprang to my eyes. What the heck was going on with me? I was never the religious type, not getting caught up in the ecstatic euphoria of it all—with Mary and the Saints and the Host, the prayers and smells and bells, and whatnot. Not like my brother Sebastian, who was the more spiritually sensitive one of the bunch. He'd be taking notes of Father Rafferty's sermons while I was blowing spit wads out of my mouth; he was busy serving at the soup kitchen while I was busy chasing girls and playing sports. Of all of us, he was the one who would've been drawn into this sort of thing I was facing. Definitely not me.

Yet there I was, eyes watering and throat constricting in on itself, being all caught up in the song, the moment of it all. If only Seba could see me now...

The singing ended, and the guys still standing for the song took their seats. A man who I assumed was the chaplain, or preacher, or priest, or whatever he was—someone in fatigues strode toward the front bearing a big book. It was black with cracked leather and crimson-stained edges, notes flopping out. The Good Book, I imagined.

I went to take an empty seat at the aisle in the back row next to someone I'd recognized but couldn't place.

"This seat open?" I asked, motioning to the thing as if the dude was saving it for his BFF.

"By all means, mate," he whispered. "Have a seat."

I smiled and nodded and took a seat. The accent sounded familiar, British and polished. While the chaplain started with some obligator remarks, I leaned in to my new row mate: "I don't normally do this sort of thing. Grew up in the Church, the Catholic Church, that is—but I don't normally do this sort of thing."

The man chuckled. "Me neither. Sort of showed up on a whim."

"Was it the singing?"

The man's smile faded. "No, it wasn't that..." He trailed off and didn't add anything further.

I didn't want to press it, but I stuck out my hand. "Silas Grey. Sergeant with the Army Rangers."

That smile returned, and he accepted. "Eli Denton. With Her Majesty's Armed Forces, the Regular Army."

"Ahh, part of the Coalition Forces. Nice to meet you. I think we slung some bullets next to one another a time or two."

"Probably. But we should also probably listen to the bloke up front," Denton said, bringing a finger to his lips. "Sounds like he's reading from the Holy Bible."

I made a zipping motion across my lips, then turned toward the man as he read:

If anyone else has reason to be confident in the flesh, I have more: circumcised on the eighth day, a member of the people of Israel, of the tribe of Benjamin, a Hebrew born of Hebrews; as to the law, a Pharisee; as to zeal, a persecutor of the church; as to righteousness under the law, blameless.

Yet whatever gains I had, these I have come to regard as loss because of Christ. More than that, I regard everything as loss because of the surpassing value of knowing Christ Jesus my Lord. For his sake I have suffered the loss of all things, and I regard them as rubbish, in order that I may gain Christ and be found in him, not having a righteousness of my own that comes from the law, but one that comes through faith in Christ, the righteousness from God based on faith. I want to know Christ and the power of his resurrection and the sharing of his sufferings by becoming like him in his death, if somehow I may attain the resurrection from the dead.

The man set his Bible on a wood lectern at the center of the front, leaving it open, a large, heavyset man with a full head of salt-and-pepper hair. I scoffed, pegging the man as one of those Jesus freaks who'd never seen combat, other than at the other end of his Bible. He began to speak—or rather, preach.

"We read here in the Book of Philippians, chapter 3, that the Apostle Paul was a man who had it all. He was of the right religion, who had done all the right rituals, and was part of the right nation. And yet, he had one thing missing."

The man paused, gripping his Bible in one hand. "Maybe you can relate, thinking that you yourself have the right pedigree. Coming from the right family, or the right state, or the right country, or the right religion. Doing all the right things, saying all the right things, learning all the right things. But what Paul describes here is the reality that Jesus is who you've been waiting for your whole life, whether you know it or not."

The man paused. A bit dramatic for my taste, but something about the way he turned that phrase struck me.

Jesus is who you've been waiting for your whole life, whether you know it or not.

"Not the right family, or the right cause, or the right religion, or right money. Jesus."

Again, the pause. Which I figured was part of his schtick, but also sensed was just part of the man's rhythm. Either way, he'd drawn me in; I was hooked.

He went on: "You see, Paul used to put his confidence in his 'flesh,' as he phrased it—his childhood faith, his adult religious zeal, his good works. But then he considered all of that a loss compared to intimately knowing God in a personal relationship. *'I want to know Christ,'* Paul had written, *'and the power of his resurrection and the sharing of his sufferings by becoming like him in his death, if somehow I may attain the resurrection from the dead.'*"

Another pause, the large man still gripping that Bible. "You see, for Paul all of who he was, all of what he had done—whether religious, or national affiliation, or familial relations. Not his past, not his pedigree, not the things that had defined him and given him worth. None of it mattered compared to Jesus!"

The chaplain paused, the seconds ticking by as he held his gaze—and our attention.

Then he continued, "Why? Because Jesus was who Paul had been waiting for his whole life, whether he knew it or not."

Something suddenly stirred inside of me. Something entirely unexpected. I couldn't describe it. Didn't make much sense, really. All I knew was that I wanted what Saint Paul had found. It was like a hunger began to well up within me, a thirst for what was standing before me—really all my life, having been raised in the Church.

"Jesus is who you've been waiting for your entire life," the chaplain repeated, "whether you know it or not."

He went on to describe the change that God works in the heart through faith in Christ: forgiveness of sins and our rebellious acts against God; release from shame and guilt; the instantaneous creation of an unbreakable, intimate relationship with the Father, sealed by the Holy Spirit; a sense of meaning and purpose at joining his mission to make things right in the world again.

The more the man spoke, the more I felt my heart strangely warmed by this unseen force. It was as if I'd been deep in the woods trudging through waist-high snow, bitter wind and a biting blizzard at my back, only to stumble across a cozy cabin with a blazing fire inside, its warmth penetrating my joints and marrow, piercing my very soul, searching and sifting the thoughts and intentions of my heart.

And what it found left me utterly exposed. Laid bare before the Lord—before all who had gathered in that tented chapel, even. It was a surreal feeling, but one thing I knew for certain: It was then, at that meeting on a base in southern Iraq, that I felt I did trust in Christ, Christ alone, for salvation. When I did, an assurance was given to me that God had taken away all of my personal baggage, my sins and hurts and habits, all that I had been carrying around all these years through childhood, since Dad's death, even the past several weeks since Colton's.

Call it a foxhole conversion, but what I saw during my years in the Middle East and what I had experienced—not only in those godforsaken desert sands, but also in that chapel—led me to seek greater meaning in my life. I realized Jesus was who he had been waiting for his whole life.

So had Denton, apparently, the man doubled over and weeping, muttering a prayer under his breath. Didn't want to disturb the man, so I let him be. But the same affection welled up within me as well.

The chaplain spoke again, bringing his message to a close. "Right now you can confess you are a rebel in need of rescue. Ask God to forgive the things you've done against him and your neighbor. Receive Jesus as your King, and trust in Jesus's death and resurrection for your own new life. If you'd like to do that now, in the quietness of this moment silently pray this prayer."

Clearing his throat, he closed his eyes and prayed aloud for us to follow:

> *God I confess that I am a rebel*
> *I've not loved you with my whole heart*
> *I've not loved my neighbor as myself*
> *I am truly sorry and I humbly turn from my way of*
> *living*
> *For the sake of Jesus Christ*
> *have mercy on me and forgive me.*
> *Jesus, I believe that you went to the cross for me and*
> *I thank you for that sacrifice.*
> *Jesus, I believe that you paid the price for my*
> *rebellion and I trust in that payment for my*
> *rescue.*
> *Jesus, I believe that God raised you from the dead*
> *and I want to experience that new life myself.*
> *Now, God, take my life, I give it to you*
> *and let it be all for you and for your glory.*
> *Amen.*

I repeated his prayer, word for word, mumbling like Denton next to me but not giving a lick if he heard me or anyone else did. Because this was between me and God. And I meant every word.

It wasn't so much that I was coming to faith the first time;

I'd done that as a young Catholic. It's that I was giving my life to Jesus, really and truly—of all places, on a military base in southern Iraq. Not because my parents told me to, or my local parish church priest. This was from the heart, my heart.

That night, I offered Christ my soul, yes, but it was more than that. I pledged him my entire life, my entire self.

The chaplain stepped back to the plate, raising his hands and saying: "This night we're here to offer Christ not only our souls, but our lives." A little too on the mark, in a mystical, almost creepy sense—given we were in the middle of a war and all—but I went with it. "So let's close by singing this song, which is really a prayer."

And off he went, inviting us to stand and giving voice to what I myself had been longing for:

> *Take my life and let it be*
> *Consecrated, Lord, to Thee.*
> *Take my moments and my days,*
> *Let them flow in endless praise.*
>
> *Take my hands and let them move*
> *At the impulse of Thy love.*
> *Take my feet and let them be*
> *Swift and beautiful for Thee.*
>
> *Take my voice and let me sing,*
> *Always, only for my King.*
> *Take my lips and let them be*
> *Filled with messages from Thee.*
>
> *Take my silver and my gold,*
> *Not a mite would I withhold.*
> *Take my intellect and use*
> *Every pow'r as Thou shalt choose.*

> *Take my will and make it Thine,*
> *It shall be no longer mine.*
> *Take my heart, it is Thine own,*
> *It shall be Thy royal throne.*
>
> *Take my love, my Lord, I pour*
> *At Thy feet its treasure store.*
> *Take myself and I will be*
> *Ever, only, all for Thee.*

"Amen," the chaplain said.

'Amen' those gathered replied loudly, retaking their seats.

"Amen..." I whispered, my throat thick with emotion to voice the truth of it. Then I wiped moisture that had congregated from my eyes and sat down.

I took in a deep breath and sighed, feeling the tightness in my chest and the heaviness from the past several weeks lift. As if my asthmatic lungs, cloudy with fluid and constricting my breath, had suddenly opened up with clarity and freedom.

I smiled at the moment, believing with every fiber of my being that I had passed over from death to life in coming to renewed faith, re-offering my intellect and will to Jesus, the product of my hands as well as my mind. Not sure what that would mean or how that would look. Maybe I'll enroll in graduate school or something, study something having to do with Christianity and the Church. Maybe even become a priest, or a minister, or whatever. Wouldn't that be something!

I chuckled at the thought, then laughed out loud. Me, a pastor? Sebastian would have a field day with that one! Not sure the pulpit and confessional was my kind of life. Maybe I could be a professor? Seemed to recall something about theology, and church history, and religious studies being offered at some of the New England schools when I was applying to undergrad.

Who knew.

What I did know was that I wanted to fight for my newfound faith! Someway, somehow. To contend for it, even. Wonder if there were any organizations I could join that were about preserving and protecting this...thing I had found?

My mind was reeling, so I slowed down. All that would come later. I took a deep breath and sighed, that final song springing back to mind.

Take my life and let it be...

I hummed it quietly as I strolled back to my barracks, humming quietly and quietly praying those words.

I chuckled again. Me, praying? Now *that* I knew Sebastian would never believe! Yet there I was, silently meditating on each stanza, praying for the wisdom and strength to reorder my hands, will, and love for the glory of God and the good of the world.

Yeah. That.

For the glory of God and good of the world...

Didn't know how that would look. Definitely not in the sands of Iraq—although, who knew? Suppose I could offer my life anywhere in the world, doing anything in the world, for God and his glory and the world's good.

I smiled, emotion again gripping my throat, eyes moistening with hope.

And that feeling again, that strange warmness. Like a blanket fresh out of the dryer, wrapping itself around me, over me, under me, inside me even.

For the first time in...well, forever, I felt free.

Which was ironic, because I had just bound myself forever to Jesus Christ, renewing the vows I had made at my profession of faith as a young Catholic, but strengthening them that evening. Then again, Jesus Christ himself promised: *'Come to me, all you who are weary and burdened, and I will give you rest. Take my yoke upon you and learn from me, for I am gentle and humble in heart, and you will find rest for your souls. For my yoke is easy and my burden is light.'*

Binding ourselves to him and his way is what we've all been searching for, whether we know it or not. Which I had done. Again, renewing my vows, if you will, from my childhood faith.

And I never looked back.

ENJOY THE STORIES?

Thanks for diving into the backstories of Silas Grey and the rest of SEPIO! Each of these characters are heroes in my *Order of Thaddeus* series. If you've missed the adventures, start today:

Holy Shroud • Book 1
The Thirteenth Apostle • Book 2
Hidden Covenant • Book 3
American God • Book 4
Grail of Power • Book 5
Templars Rising • Book 6
Rite of Darkness • Book 7
Gospel Zero • Book 8
The Emperor's Code • Book 9
Strange Blessing • Book 10

Enjoy the story? Here's what you can do next:

If you loved the book and have a moment to spare, **a short review is much appreciated.** Nothing fancy, just your honest take. Spreading the word is probably the #1 way you can help independent authors like me and help others enjoy the story.

If you're ready for another adventure, you can get a full-length novel in the series for free! All you have to do is join the insider's group to be notified of specials and new releases by going to this link: www.jabouma.com/free

You might also like my apocalyptic sci-fi thriller series, *Ichthus Chronicles.* Set 100 years in the future, the last remnant of Christianity is threatened from forces inside and outside the Church, written in the vein of the *Left Behind* series. Start the adventure today: www.jabouma.com/books/apostasy-rising-1

GET YOUR FREE THRILLER

Building a relationship with my readers is one of my all-time favorite joys of writing! Once in a while I like to send out a newsletter with giveaways, free stories, pre-release content, updates on new books, and other bits on my stories.

Join my insider's group for updates, giveaways, and your free novel—a full-length action-adventure story in my *Order of Thaddeus* thriller series. Just tell me where to send it.

Follow this link to subscribe:
www.jabouma.com/free

ALSO BY J. A. BOUMA

J. A. Bouma believes nobody should have to read bad religious fiction —whether it's cheesy plots with pat answers or misrepresentations of the Christian faith and the Bible. So he wants to do something about it by telling compelling, propulsive stories that thrill as much as inspire, while offering a dose of insight along the way.

Order of Thaddeus Action-Adventure Thriller Series

Holy Shroud • Book 1

The Thirteenth Apostle • Book 2

Hidden Covenant • Book 3

American God • Book 4

Grail of Power • Book 5

Templars Rising • Book 6

Rite of Darkness • Book 7

Gospel Zero • Book 8

The Emperor's Code • Book 9

Silas Grey Collection 1 (Books 1-3)

Silas Grey Collection 2 (Books 4-6)

Silas Grey Collection 3 (Books 7-9)

Short Story Collection 1

Ichthus Chronicles Sci-Fi Apocalyptic Series

Apostasy Rising / Season 1, Episode 1

Apostasy Rising / Season 1, Episode 2

Apostasy Rising / Season 1, Episode 3

Apostasy Rising / Season 1, Episode 4

Apostasy Rising / Full Season 1 (Episodes 1 to 4)

Apocalypse Rising / Season 2, Episode 1

Apocalypse Rising / Season 2, Episode 2

Apocalypse Rising / Season 2, Episode 3

Apocalypse Rising / Season 2, Episode 4

Apocalypse Rising / Full Season

Faith Reimagined **Spiritual Coming-of-Age Series**

A Reimagined Faith • Book 1

A Rediscovered Faith • Book 2

A Ruined Faith • Book 3 (2020)

A Resurrected Faith • Book 4 (2021)

Mill Creek Junction **Short Story Series**

Get all the latest short stories at: www.millcreekjunction.com

Find all of my latest book releases at: www.jabouma.com

ABOUT THE AUTHOR

J. A. Bouma believes nobody should have to read bad religious fiction--whether it's cheesy plots with pat answers or misrepresentations of the Christian faith and the Bible. So he wants to do something about it by telling compelling, propulsive stories that thrill as much as inspire, while offering a dose of insight along the way.

As a former congressional staffer and pastor, and award-nominated bestselling author of over forty religious fiction and nonfiction books, he blends a love for ideas and adventure, exploration and discovery, thrill and thought. With graduate degrees in Christian thought and the Bible, and armed with a voracious appetite for most mainstream genres, he tells stories you'll read with abandon and recommend with pride—exploring the tension of faith and doubt, spirituality and culture, belief and practice, and the gritty drama that is our collective pilgrim story.

When not putting fingers to keyboard, he loves vintage jazz vinyl, a glass of Malbec, and an epic read—preferably together. He lives in Grand Rapids with his wife, two kiddos, and rambunctious boxer-pug-terrier.

www.jabouma.com • jeremy@jabouma.com

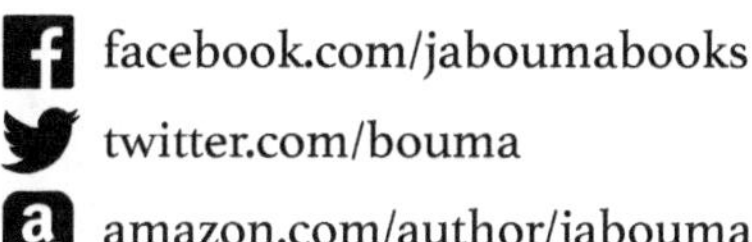

facebook.com/jaboumabooks
twitter.com/bouma
amazon.com/author/jabouma